AN EVANS NOVEL OF THE WEST

LAKOTA

G. CLIFTON WISLER

M. EVANS & COMPANY, INC.   NEW YORK

Library of Congress Cataloging-in-Publication Data

Wisler, G. Clifton.

   Lakota / G. Clifton Wisler.
     p.   cm. — (An Evans novel of the West)
   ISBN 0-87131-563-7
   1. Lakota Indians—Fiction.   I. Title.   II. Series.
   PS3573.I877L35 1989 89-1498
   813'.54—dc20

M. Evans and Company, Inc.
216 East 49 Street
New York, New York 10017

Manufactured in the United States of America

9 8 7 6 5 4 3 2 1

In grateful appreciation,
Lakota *is dedicated to*
Victor, Lionel, and
my other friends at Sinte Gleska College
and among the Sicangu Lakota people

Chapter One

They called themselves Lakota for the branch of the tribal language spoken by the seven southern bands. The white man called them Teton Sioux, the prairie dwellers, and spoke the name with a mixture of dread and respect. They were the fiercest hunters and the most unrelenting of enemies. But all that was yet to come. For in the year marked by the black robe priests 1848, under the greenleaf moon of May, bands of the tribe knew only the peace of fattening ponies and mild weather.

In Little Thunder's camp, deep in Pe Sla, the circular valley that is the heart of Paha Sapa, the Black Hills, the people were restless. There, in that sacred place which is the center of the earth, Tasiyagnunpa, the Meadowlark, felt the pains of birthing beginning. As her female relatives offered prayers and provided what comfort experience had taught, Tacante, the father, climbed a distant slope in search of a dreaming.

For Tacante, it was not the first time he had awaited a child's coming into the light. Twice before Tasiyagnunpa's belly had grown large. Each time a small, sickly thing had emerged, only to close its eyes in the silent death understood only by the grandfathers' grandfathers.

"Sing the brave song, my brother," Hinhan Hota, the Gray Owl, had urged. "There is much that isn't understood."

"Han," Tacante had sadly agreed. Yes, Wakan Tanka, the Great

1

Mystery, gave life only to take it away again. Who could understand that?

Each time Tacante grieved for the dead ones three days, even as he had mourned for a father and a mother taken by winter's chill. Now, as he climbed the rocky hillside, his heart sang with new hope.

"Wakan Tanka, hear me," he pleaded. "I have danced and I have smoked. I have undertaken Inipi, the purification rite, and even now I starve myself as I did long ago in the time of my coming upon manhood. Always I am generous to the needy. I hunt so that the people grow strong, and I have never neglected to pray and smoke before going upon the hunt."

Tacante paused and stared out at the darkening skies. Soon the sacred hoop of stars, Can Gleska Wakan, would appear high overhead and bring the earth back to life from the depths of winter's death. Surely this was a time of birth. Down below Tasiyagnunpa struggled to give him a son. But it would live only if Wakan Tanka so willed it.

"I am called Tacante," he spoke as he removed his buckskin shirt, then stepped free of his moccasins. He continued stripping until he stood naked before the Great Mystery, a man free of pride and bare of pretensions. "I ask a son, Wakan Tanka, a brave one to follow the sacred path behind me. He Hopa, who has great power, says I will not live long if I walk the warrior path. It is the only path a man can walk who has been given the name Tacante."

He stopped a moment and gazed at the evening star sparkling on the horizon. It was true. Tacante meant Buffalo Heart, but it might as well have been spoken Heart of the People. One so named must always ride first into battle, must always put the needs of the people ahead of his own. He had been a shirt wearer four winters now, and the scars on his chest and thighs attested to his courage. Tacante now added to those scars, for he drew his knife and cut the flesh of his chest four times. Blood seeped from the wounds and dripped down his bare trunk, across his thighs, and down his legs. He sang a brave song and chanted boldly.

"Ah, Wakan Tanka, grant my prayer. Send to me a brave heart to endure what will come. May a son come tonight to the Lakota people, one with the heart to lead others and the power to see danger. Ah, Wakan Tanka, walk with me these short days of my life. All that is flows from your power. Help me to walk the sacred way."

2

Tacante chanted and sang, turning slowly so that the darkness above could see the blood flowing from him. To the Great Mystery he prayed and pleaded. Then, as his strength began to ebb, he sank to his knees, then passed into the peace of dreaming.

In the silent, hollow darkness of the netherworld, Tacante saw many things. First there came a great marching of storm clouds. Thunderbird flapped its wings, and yellow tongues of lightning danced across the heavens, stinging Mother Earth and causing her to tremble. Into this scene crept Tatanka, Bull Buffalo. He was not the tall, humped master of the yellowing plain as in the past, though. Tatanka stood on the prairie amid the storm, and tears fell from his somber eyes. Before him stretched a sea of whitening bones, for his brothers lay slaughtered in their hundreds. Only bones remained to haunt the valleys.

"Our path is a short one, Tacante, my brother," Bull Buffalo spoke. And even as Tatanka howled a death chant, the rumbling thunder tormented him with its yellow daggers.

Tacante awoke hours later. He Hopa, Four Horns, the medicine man of great power, dabbed yellow paste on Tacante's wounds.

"You've had a dreaming?" the old man asked.

"Hau, a dark dream, He Hopa," Tacante answered. He then described the vision, and the medicine man frowned.

"Ah, you've seen much," He Hopa observed.

"What does it mean?" Tacante asked.

"Much, perhaps. Or little."

"Tell me."

"There is much death to come. The buffalo will die, and with him the Lakota."

"This can't be," Tacante objected. "There are more buffalo on the earth than stars in the heavens. Tatanka is our uncle. He feeds and clothes the people. He is for all times."

"Ah, have you not seen how the rocks of Paha Sapa break apart in the grip of winter? Only Father Sky and Mother Earth live long. All else walks a path. Short or long, who can say?"

"And what am I to do, He Hopa? I am but a single Lakota."

"You're a shirt wearer, Tacante," He Hopa scolded. "You must see to the welfare of the people."

"If such hard times are ahead, I will need help."

"Then ask Wakan Tanka that the son born this night be strong and swift and wise. For surely Tasiyagnunpa brings a boy into your lodge. I, too, have dreams."

"Yes," Tacante said, raising his arms skyward and chanting the required prayers. He turned slowly and sang. He Hopa joined in, shaking a rattlesnake charm in one hand while clutching the sacred medicine bags in the other. And then, swift as a red-tailed hawk dives upon his prey, the old medicine man halted.

"Dress yourself, Tonska," He Hopa commanded. "Your son awaits you, Nephew."

Tacante raised a howl of thanksgiving and then uttered a short prayer. After dressing himself, he hurried back to the camp.

Tasiyagnunpa remained in the women's lodge, among the grandmothers, but Wablosa, Redwing Blackbird, her mother's sister, emerged from the lodge with a tiny bundle.

"Cinks?" Tacante asked. My son?

Wablosa nodded, then showed the child to its father. Tacante touched the infant's tiny, whitish hands and stroked the raven-black hairs on its head.

"Ah, Tacante, a son," He Hopa observed. "What will he be called?"

"I had thought 'Little Heart,' or 'Buffalo Calf,' as I myself was called."

"He hasn't the look of a buffalo," Wablosa joked. "The grandmothers have named him Mastincala."

"Rabbit's a good name for one so light-skinned," He Hopa declared.

"A hard name to wear among the foxes and elks," Tacante complained. "I've dreamed. I saw thunder."

"Yes, Tonska, but the dream was for you, not him. Mastincala is a good name. Perhaps Rabbit will give him speed and cunning. There is time yet for Tatanka to visit his dreams."

Tacante dropped his head in disappointment. And yet his frown did not linger. The child gazed up with mystified eyes, and buffalo heart or no, a father's pride swelled within him. He touched the baby boy on the forehead and silently pledged all the devotion a father could offer.

You will be proud one day to walk the sacred path with me, Mastincala, Tacante promised. And proud, too, to be the son of a shirt wearer.

4

Chapter Two

Mastincala, the rabbit boy, learned early the lessons life taught a Lakota child. When the urge to cry came upon him, Wablosa pinched his nose and covered his mouth until tiny lungs burned with the need for air.

"There, little one," his aunt would scold. "See how it is death to cry out? Would you give away a silent camp to our enemies?"

The infant couldn't understand the words, but he soon learned the futility of wailing. Once, while the band was erecting its tipis, he cried to attract attention. Tacante promptly carried his cradleboard beyond hearing and left him to howl to himself. No sooner did he stop than old Wablosa appeared to tend him. By and by, as his needs were met by Wablosa, Tasiyagnunpa, or some female cousin or aunt, he learned instinctively to trust that all would be tended in time.

He spent his early days strapped in a cradleboard, bouncing along on his mother's back as the camp moved out onto the plains in search of Uncle Tatanka, Bull Buffalo. Other days, when the band encamped near some stream or beside a spring in the hills, he would crawl about, discovering the freedom of the camp. Other children would often play tricks on him or roll a buckskin ball to him. Sometimes he would creep over among the elders. They would not scold him or chase him back to the children. Sometimes old He Hopa, Four Horns, the medicine man, would speak strange words and draw the boy child close.

"Ah, see how Mastincala seeks the wisdom of his elders," the old man told his fellows. "He will grow to be a shirt wearer like his father. Or else be a man of power like this old grandfather."

He Hopa presented Mastincala a medicine bundle when next the child crawled to the old men's fire, and the others howled their approval as the Rabbit clutched a sacred horn.

"See," He Hopa cried. "He is already the man of power I foresaw."

The other men laughed at the thought of an infant knowing the sacred ways of Wakan Tanka. But they took new interest in the restless one.

Mastincala enjoyed his wanderings. Most of the time, that is. The time he crawled into the coals of his father's fire, he screamed in pain. The tender skin of his hands was scorched most severely, and as he fled the fiery earth, he stared at the amused faces of those he judged his protectors.

"See there, Mastincala, foolish one," Tacante said. "You've burned yourself. A wise man doesn't put his hands in the fire."

Wablosa then carried him to He Hopa's lodge, and the medicine man provided a thick yellow paste that soothed the burned hands.

It was the way a boy learned best, so said the Lakota elders. Leave a child to burn himself, and he will not need to be told a fire is hot. Leave the anxious mind to explore. He will learn.

And so Mastincala took his first steps when he undertook the notion to walk. He spoke as he grew able to form the words. His questions were answered if it wasn't inconvenient, and understanding began to supplant impulse.

By the time he greeted his seventh summer, he knew much. He could easily recognize the dress and traditions of his band, the Sicangu Lakota, the burned-thigh people or Brules, as the French traders knew them. He could quite naturally tell the difference between his Oglala cousins and the Pawnees or the Crows, their enemies. He sensed his father was a great man, for even the head man of the band, Little Thunder, would seek the counsel of the man known as Buffalo Heart. Tacante's prestige flowed from the beaded shirt he wore when leading raids upon the Pawnee horse herds or while chasing curious Crows from the buffalo range.

He learned, too, the heavy burdens life placed on the shoulders of an only son. For in those seven years three times Tasiyagnunpa had walked heavy with child, but only once did the infant live. And Mastincala had little use for the pudgy sister that was named Wicatankala, Gull. She soon grew nearly as tall as her brother, and she had not half the trouble with her name the rabbit had with his.

Yes, Mastincala found his name a trial. While he shot small, blunt-pointed arrows with the other boys, they teased him beyond all reason. How was it a rabbit should walk among Little Raven or Mountain Hawk? There were boys named for beavers and eagles and horses. And there was the one called Rabbit.

"Ah," He Hopa assured Mastincala, "one day you will be a man of power. Those others will hunt and live and die, but they will follow you in time of trial. It is good that a man who would lead the people should face hardships. You must make a prayer of thanks to Wakan Tanka, who sends you this struggle to make you strong."

Mastincala did so, but it was hard to feel glad when the sharp words of the other boys stung his seven-year-old heart. And while Wicatankala doted upon her skinny, pale-skinned brother, the other girls enjoyed teasing the Rabbit.

"Take care no hawk swoops down and takes you off to Paha Sapa," they called.

"No, hawks see good," Capa, the Beaver, observed. "He is too little to make a meal of. Even a Pawnee would not waste an arrow on him."

The others laughed, and Mastincala suffered.

He might have endured the name and his slow growth more easily were it not for the light pigment of his skin. Others, whose flesh had grown dark brown, spoke of the white rabbit. When wagons of the Wasicun, the white people, passed along the road they had built beside the Platte, they often spoke to him in their stranger tongues.

"They want to know if you have a white mother or father," some trader's son translated.

Mastincala replied in his shrill voice that he was Sicangu Lakota, the son of Tacante, the great hunter and shirt wearer.

But still the whites wished to take him from his people, to see him placed among the black robe priests who came among the Lakota with their loud words of the angry wakan. These whites were a strange people, Mastincala decided. They had many laws that were never to be broken, and yet they needed many soldiers to chase down those who broke such laws. At the forts there were lodges with iron windows where men who violated the laws were kept. Even soldiers were locked in those lodges. How much simpler to take the Lakota way. A man or woman who did wrong was sent from the camp. Was there worse pain than being taken from the people, left to wander the earth alone?

And yet being among the white people was not altogether bad. They had many good things to trade for buffalo hides. Tacante and other warriors boasted fine rifles. The traders and the wagon travelers, too, would give many fine beads and much cloth for fresh trout plucked from the river or even a pair of worn moccasins. And while among the whites, Mastincala's skin appeared not so pale.

At one fort, the one called Laramie, Mastincala met the first great friend of his young life. This was Hinkpila, Short Hair, also called Louis Le Doux by the whites. His skin was dark for a white man, and Hinkpila explained how his grandmother was a Lakota. Hinkpila was of an age and size to be Mastincala's twin, and the two boys, both misfits among their own people, spent many days swimming the river, wrestling on the sandy banks, or racing through cottonwood groves that stood between the Sicangu camp and the white man's fort.

It was as good a time as a boy not old enough to ride to the buffalo hunt might know, but it didn't last forever. A year had passed since a soldier chief had fired upon Conquering Bear's camp, and the Lakota had fought a battle near the fort. Many soldiers had been slain, for Conquering Bear had been killed and the people were very angry. Peace followed, but now Hinkpila's father brought word the soldiers were angry with the Lakota and were sending an eagle chief to teach the Indian a lesson.

"We will go," Tacante explained to his son. "We've always known Le Doux to give us good words. We have traded, and now we should seek out Uncle Tatanka."

So Mastincala bid his friend farewell, leaving him the gift of a fine buffalo-hide coat to mark their friendship.

"White men make poor coats," the Rabbit declared. "This will keep you warm when the snows come."

In return, Hinkpila gave his Lakota friend a fine steel knife with a polished bone handle. It was a knife to put Capa and his friends to shame, and Mastincala rode eastward along the Platte road feeling taller and prouder. But his heart was sad, too, for he had never parted with a friend before.

That summer was a remembered time for Little Thunder's Sicangus. Good fortune smiled on the hunt, and soon the camp was alive with the aroma of smoking meat. Bellies were full, and as the grandmothers pounded chokecherries into strips of meat to make the wasna, the dried buffalo meat that would prevent winter starving, songs of thanks rose to Wakan Tanka.

Mastincala was too young to ride with the hunters, but he stalked what game was to be found beside Platte River. His first kill was a plump porcupine, and his mother accepted it proudly. Quills were greatly favored for decorating warrior shirts, after all.

Soon thereafter the Rabbit had his first spirit dreaming. Often he had seen images of this or that in his sleep, but never had the spirit visions seemed as real. He sought out He Hopa and explained about the dream, telling how while he had been hunting with the other boys in the rocks beyond the river, a large black bear had come upon them. It growled and fell upon them, striking boys until none save Mastincala remained. The bear had gazed with cold eyes upon the Rabbit while the boy notched an arrow and let it fly into the bear's heart.

"Ah, brave one, I am no more," the bear had cried. Then he was gone, and the boys were alive once more.

"Perhaps your heart is torn by the words of your brothers, little one," He Hopa said, leading the boy aside. "You are seen small and unworthy by their eyes, and you wish to grow taller."

"It's true," Mastincala admitted. "But the bear felt close."

"Then perhaps he will come, and you will have your chance," He Hopa said, smiling. "Here, I will give you a strong arrow with a sharp point. Carry it among your deer arrows."

Mastincala thanked the medicine man for the gift, and Four Horns urged caution.

"Maybe it is only a dream," the old man said. "But your eyes have always held power, Mastincala. The bear may come."

Mastincala spoke to no one else of the bear or the dream, not even his father. In time he put it out of his mind. To the other boys, he made up one tale after another to explain the long, sharp-pointed arrow he carried in his quiver. But despite their nagging, he never once spoke of the truth.

"A man of power should not betray his secrets," He Hopa said often. It was wisdom well spoken, for Mastincala couldn't have endured the taunts that would have followed a seven-year-old's revelation of a spirit dream.

Then one afternoon as the boys stalked a small doe in the rocks beyond the river, they came upon a rockslide. As they crept among the fallen boulders and passed a dark hole in the hillside, a roar not unlike thunder froze their feet. Out of the darkness rumbled the very bear Mastincala had seen in his dream.

"Run!" Capa screamed as he scampered away from the lumbering creature. Those who could did so. Two of the older ones fired arrows first. Their small shafts and flint points, designed to penetrate bird feathers or rabbit fur, bounced harmlessly off the enormous bulk of the bear. Both shooters were suddenly in terrible peril. That was when Mastincala called to the bear.

"Here I am, Mato! I, Mastincala, am ready for you."

The bear turned and eyed the bare-chested boy as Mastincala notched his arrow. Then, holding his arm as steady as was possible, the Rabbit let loose his arrow. It struck the bear in the throat. The animal roared in pain and bellowed so that the earth began to shake. The terrified boys fled through the rocks, all save Mastincala, who remained to await his fate. Suddenly Tacante and his brother, Hinhan Hota, arrived. They leveled their new rifles and fired. The bear fell on its side and breathed out its life.

The boys howled their relief, then raced to touch their bows to the flanks of the fallen bear, thus counting coup on the enemy. Mastincala stood as before, solitary and silent. His ears filled with the remembered dream voice of the bear, and he knew a great moment had come to him.

Tacante saw the strange gaze of his son and led the boy finally away from the bear. Only then did Mastincala tell of the dream and of He Hopa's counsel.

"Ah, it was a brave thing, little one," Tacante declared. "But very dangerous. It's a shirt wearer's duty to come to the aid of his brothers, but to stand and die is never desired. A man can't help his family if he dies young."

Mastincala felt the comfort of his father's strong arm and rejoiced that he had Buffalo Heart for a protector. Hinhan Hota later dragged the dead bear to the camp, and the band enjoyed a feasting that night. As for the skin, Hinhan Hota promised Mastincala a fine winter coat from it.

Such a day would have been remembered even if He Hopa had not risen that night to speak to the people.

"I have said here is a boy with power to see things," the medicine man reminded them. "Now he has stood as a warrior and protected his brothers. Surely there would be the wail of burial songs among us tonight if not for Mastincala's courage. It is a brave deed he has done, and I say it now to all."

The others murmured their agreement. Even Capa and the other boys whooped and beat small sticks together in recognition of the Rabbit's deed.

He Hopa then motioned Mastincala to come close, and the old man produced an eagle feather and tied it in the boy's hair.

"Here has been done the first of many brave deeds," He Hopa announced. "Wakan Tanka, watch over this little one that he may grow tall in wisdom. May his feet never stray from the sacred path."

The others howled their agreement, and Mastincala stretched himself to his full height and grinned back at his assembled admirers. Such moments don't last long, he knew, and are best enjoyed at the moment. Tomorrow would bring new tasks and fresh undertakings. There would be rest only tonight.

Chapter Three

Rabbit is a clever creature. He dwells in the roughest hollows, among the thorny bushes and the cacti. He builds his warren beneath the earth, in places overlooked and ignored by most men and safe from the keen eyes of the soaring hawks. He is never content with a solitary entrance. He digs a second so as to provide always a lane of escape. And while foraging for his sustenance, he often retraces his steps, thus making a double trail that leads in a circle. Even the best Lakota trackers admitted Rabbit was clever.

From Tacante, Mastincala learned to observe his brother creatures, especially Rabbit.

"You may be small," his father taught, "but so is Rabbit. See how he goes where the fox cannot follow. He has no bow or knife, yet he wounds those who would bring his death. Learn this lesson, little one."

Mastincala watched the other creatures, too. Antelope showed how the fleet might escape harm. Fox taught the patience of a good hunter. Bear used his great power and stamina. And Uncle Buffalo, he that was sacred above all creatures, showed how one walked the sacred path, taking only what was needed and giving in return what he could.

He Hopa took great interest in Mastincala, and the medicine man devoted many days to teaching the lore of the tribe. Sometimes the two would walk beside the river and share some story of the long-ago times. Mastincala took each word of those tales to heart, for there were lessons within. And when He Hopa showed which roots or moss could take the fever from the sick, or where the sacred medicine paint came from, Mastincala remembered. Knowledge brought power. This much he knew as a boy in his seventh summer.

From the time of the bear dreaming, Tacante looked at his son with new pride. Now, when the band moved after the buffalo, Mastincala was sometimes allowed to ride with the men, out ahead on a scout, or perhaps to hunt game for the supper kettle. Tacante and Hinhan Hota, the Gray Owl, often fought mock battles with the boy or wrestled with him in the deer meadows. Hinhan Hota showed Mastincala a fine new bow cut from the sacred wood of the ash.

"This bow will be yours, my son," his uncle said, for in the Lakota way, a father's brothers are one's fathers also. "When you can pull the bowstring, then we will set off into the thickets after deer."

"Will that be soon?" Mastincala asked.

"Soon," Hinhan Hota answered, lifting the boy onto one shoulder. "The moon will be born whole and be eaten many times before you have the arm to pull the string. Your heart would pull it now."

"I'm but a rabbit among boys," Mastincala complained.

"Remember, little one, rabbit is clever. And the arm will grow larger and stronger. Others may pull it before you, but they won't have the true aim that lies in your eye. Who among them struck bear? Hau! Whose heart is greater than Mastincala?"

The boy grew warm in the glow of such praise. It wasn't often the Owl spoke such words, for it was Hinhan Hota of all the men who undertook Mastincala's education in the ritual and rule of the Lakota camp. Too often Gray Owl sternly scolded Mastincala for teasing his sister or speaking to his mother.

"You are old enough to begin walking a man's path," Hinhan Hota declared. "From this time you must address Tasiyagnunpa, your mother, only through others. Your sister, Wicatankala, must be treated much the same. It is hard for one without brothers. But Tasiyagnunpa, your mother, is young. Perhaps one day you will call someone *Misun.*"

Brother? Mastincala considered the matter cautiously. After all, brothers had been born before, but the light quickly left their eyes.

"Yes, Hinhan Hota," Mastincala finally said. "A brother would help with the labors. I could teach him many things, even as you have shown me. I have no friends among the other boys. They say I am white, like a winter rabbit, even after my skin has grown dark and brown from the summer's sun."

"The spirits send trials to make you strong."

"Ah, so many?" the boy asked. "When the time of the hunt is over, maybe Hinkpila Le Doux can come to our camp. There is room in my father's lodge."

"Perhaps," Hinhan Hota agreed. "When the eagle chief has no more anger against our people, we will surely visit the fort again. You and he can teach each other much."

"And I can wrestle Hinkpila to the ground," Mastincala boasted. "As one day I will do with you."

"Ah, when Tatanka has crushed my bones and time has wrinkled my hide. Only then!" Hinhan Hota declared. "Only then."

Talk of Louis warmed the Rabbit. He looked fondly upon the end of the hunting days. The camp was forever on the move, and everyone was weary from work. There were so many hides to work already, and the meat was still drying on the racks, those strips not snatched by prank-playing boys or prowling animals. And he, Mastincala, rabbit boy, was forever in the company of his jeering fellows, boys like Capa who stood half a head taller. Ah, Mastincala thought, how sharp the tongues of boys can be!

The hunt was over soon, but it ended in far from the ordinary way. The Lakota were camped on Blue Creek, in a place the white men in their wheeled lodges called Ash Hollow. Fools they were, those whites, Mastincala thought as he tended his father's horses. There were not ash trees there at all!

It was a well-traveled spot, however, for there the wagon trains descended a high bluff in order to follow the North Platte to Fort Laramie. Many of the whites seemed ill at ease, seeing Little Thunder's Lakotas camping so near, and they often shot off their guns to warn away Lakotas who went to trade for tobacco or lead. Sometimes a young man's blood would rise, and he would steal a horse from the wagon people.

Such unauthorized raids were a bad business. The whites grew angry, and perhaps they would shoot more often as they passed through this Lakota country. Le Doux said the soldier chiefs were angry and sent many men. He had told of how the little soldier chief at Laramie had slain Conquering Bear and others because of a single cow. Would they not be more angry over the theft of horses?

As it happened, the soldiers did come. Mastincala knew not whether the wagon people sent word of Little Thunder's camp or whether the Pawnees, who often scouted for the bluecoats, sent the eagle chief Harney upon the old enemy. It mattered little. One night Mastincala lay as always in the soft elk robe beside his father in the lodge painted with the magic buffalo figures revealed in his father's dreamings. The next morning the sky split open, and thunder exploded through the world.

Mastincala knew nothing of war. Once he had looked into He Hopa's medicine lodge when a young man caught in a buffalo stampede was brought inside. The young Lakota had lain there, his body battered and broken, the blood dried brown on his chest and trunk. The buffalo had crushed him as a man stepping upon a pine cone broke it into pieces, and death quickly arrived.

Now, as the eagle chief's thunder guns breathed fire, whole lodges exploded. Lodge poles as thick as a man's waist snapped like twigs. Proud warriors were ripped apart like dolls made of cornstalks.

"Take your sister, Mastincala, my son," Tacante shouted as he dragged them both from the lodge. "Be a rabbit, little one. Run so that the bluecoats have no eyes with which to find you."

Mastincala thought to argue. He didn't want to run away with the women and little ones. His was the warrior's path. But Tacante waved his hand angrily at the scattering camp, at the dust rising beneath the wasicuns' horses.

"Go, my son!" Buffalo Heart cried, his eyes pleading more than ordering. "I am a shirt wearer and must look to the others. Be brave, little one. Look to your sister."

Mastincala waved Wicatankala along as he darted between the fiery mountains of black smoke. His sister fought to keep pace, but she often stumbled and fell. He muttered under his breath and pulled her along. At the edge of camp, He Hopa and others of the old men were collecting the helpless ones. Mastincala left his sister among them and started back into the battle-torn camp.

There was nothing so lovely as the circle of conical tipis that formed a Lakota camp. Little Thunder's band took great pride in its lodges, and many were brightly painted with scenes of courage and triumph. Now a storm of fire devoured half those lodges, and the surviving ones witnessed a scene of pitiless butchery. Soldiers rode their ponies down on the mystified band of men, women, and children. Capa, who had been among the worst of Mastincala's tormentors, stood bravely before a white soldier. The Beaver was yet to see his ninth winter, nor would he. The bluecoat fired a rifle bullet through one ear, and Capa fell.

For the first time Mastincala sensed the dark despair of approaching death. If a black cloud had swallowed the world, it could not have brought more darkness to his mind. Two women fought to save their blankets from a burning lodge. Soldiers shot them down, then threw them back into the burning tipi.

Mastincala froze as he saw Hinhan Hota. The Owl was hurrying a handful of little ones from the camp while firing his rifle at any white men who approached too closely.

"Run, little one!" Gray Owl shouted at his nephew. "Run!"

"I can fight," Mastincala argued. "There is the bow."

"There is a day to fight and a day to run!" Hinhan Hota yelled.

Even as the owl spoke, a wild-eyed soldier charged the fleeing children. Gray Owl fired, and the soldier's head snapped back.

The little ones fled toward the creek as Hinhan Hota worked to reload the rifle. A thin blue line of riflemen now appeared. Gray Owl threw himself on the ground as a storm of lead swept the scene. Bullets impacted on buffalo hides or lodge poles, causing sounds like the beating of blankets by old women. Another lodge fell.

The air suddenly filled with the buzzing of hornets, or so it seemed to Mastincala. A woman fell back across a cradleboard peppered with shot. Her daughter died a good Lakota, never crying out with the pain that came with the bullet. An invisible hammer then pounded Mastincala's left elbow, and he fell.

The world was like a dream now. He looked at his arm as blood dug channels through the grime. Pain erupted from his splintered elbow, and for a moment he thought his arm was likely to fall off. He clasped a reassuring right hand against the wound and saw the ball had passed on through after breaking the bone. Only then, as he searched for a strip of cloth or buckskin to bind the wound, did he realize he stood barefoot and near naked.

He crawled along the ground, finally stopping when he reached the body of the wasicun killed by Hinhan Hota. The soldier wore a fresh cloth shirt, and Mastincala had no trouble tearing it into the required strips. He then crawled onward, hoping to spy the Owl up ahead. He saw only soldiers firing volleys into a circle of Lakotas who were trying to hold the far side of the camp. Behind them the last of the women and children not escaped or killed huddled together in fear.

Mastincala couldn't help feeling proud of his people. There was only death awaiting those warriors, but they would not save themselves and leave the helpless ones to die. Two men stood tallest. Both wore warrior shirts. The first to fall was Tacante. Then the soldiers simply overran the others, and the dying took a few moments longer.

"Ah, Ate," Mastincala wailed. He made the brave song of the warriors and pleaded with Wakan Tanka to make his father's spirit path an easy one. The boy was dizzy with loss of blood, and his heart was rent in two. Nevertheless he managed to stand and watch the women and little ones racing past soldiers too consumed with looting the camp to notice them.

"Hau, Wakan Tanka," Mastincala called as he traced streaks of red down his face and chest with bloodstained fingers. "It's a good day to die, Tacante. I join you."

But the soldiers had no eyes to see the boy among them. His fiery eyes stabbed them, and his heart erased them from that insane world. But the Rabbit was nothing to trouble with, after all. They left him to wander the camp, listening to the dying chants and final mumblings of Little Thunder's people.

Mastincala knelt beside his father. Tacante's bared chest showed two holes, and another shot had pierced his hip. The shirt Tacante had been so proud to wear would now remind some wasicun of the treacherous attack on a peaceful people.

Ate, Mastincala said silently. *Father, I would have died with you, but the wasicun won't honor me with a warrior's death. The time will come when they will be sorry. They, too, will bleed.*

He felt a strong hand grip his shoulder. A white-haired wasicun stared down with strange, somehow sorrowful eyes. He spoke words beyond

Mastincala's understanding. The boy knew only a smattering of English from his time in the fort. He recalled a single word only.

"Father," Mastincala explained.

The white-haired man barked at a party of soldiers who were busy collecting discarded guns. One trotted over, threw Mastincala over his shoulder, and started toward a pair of four-wheeled wagons rolling toward the creek. Mastincala kicked and struggled to free himself, but the wasicun was young and strong. His grip was iron.

I am but a rabbit, Mastincala told himself. *Helpless. But later there will come a time. Then I will dig my hole and escape these blue-coated devils.*

The sun marched slowly across the great blue sky that day, but even the amber glow of dusk failed to end the people's suffering. Among the Lakota survivors were many wounded. Others wailed the funeral song for the brave dead. In another time men would have hacked willow limbs to make travois for the wounded or to build scaffolds upon which to lay the dead. The soldiers took even the small bows of the youngest child, though, and a band of bluecoats prevented their captives from crossing the creek and visiting the slain.

Tacante should have rested in a high place, surrounded by his painted shield and an ash bow. It grieved Mastincala to know his father lay untended. The wasicun eagle chief, the one called Harney, had ordered the camp burned, and the possessions accumulated by three generations were swept into memory by curling tails of black smoke. Some of the corpses were burned as well. A few were covered with earth in the white man's way. Most were left to feed the birds.

Harney wasn't concerned with the dead. In truth, he seemed to have little pity upon the living. He soon ordered the survivors to move along Platte River, and his soldiers saw it done. Those too weak to walk were carried by their weary companions. The strong helped the weak. Soon, though, there were few strong ones left. The Gray Owl, Hinhan Hota, and many of the younger warriors had escaped death and fled into the hills. A few wandered in, surrendered their weapons, and joined the sad caravan. Hinhan Hota didn't.

"So long as a single Lakota lives, so our people live," He Hopa sang.

Mastincala tried to put on a brave face, knowing his father's brother, his second ate, was out among the wild things, maybe riding his horse where the buffalo still shook the earth. It was a hard thing, being brave. He gazed at the dark brown stains on the white bandage a wasicun medicine chief had put on his elbow. His whole arm hurt, but he musn't show it. He was a man now, as other boys among the Sicangu were men. They guarded their sad-eyed mothers and sisters, knowing it would be hard to follow the sacred path with no fathers to guide them.

There were some men in the camp, though. A handful had suffered only slight wounds. Others had been surprised in their beds by soldiers who lacked the wolf's hungry eye. Death had satisfied its appetite elsewhere. A few had gone to guard the women, old ones mostly, or boys not yet allowed to ride to the buffalo hunt. Among a band of children, a boy of fourteen snows seemed tall indeed.

For most, the greatest fear lay ahead. It wasn't easy facing the great unknown. What fate did these wasicun chiefs have in mind for the captives? Were the women to be taken into some chief's lodge, as was the fashion of the Pawnees and Crows? Would the youngest boys be adopted?

When asked these questions by those Lakotas who spoke English words, soldiers laughed. They told tales of hanging men by the necks from trees or throwing them in small iron boxes. Some said the women would be given to the Pawnee scouts. Others told how boys were flayed with rawhide strips until their flesh cracked and bled. Terrible mutilations were performed. After such tales, some boys always fled the camp, and the soldier chiefs ordered the talking stopped. Some of the fugitive Lakotas were recaptured, but not many were not.

"I, too, should run away," Mastincala told old He Hopa. "I can find Hinhan Hota, my uncle-father. He will come to slay the wasicuns."

"No, Tonska," Four Horns warned. "There are a hundred times the fingers of my hands of these wasicuns. You would take the fever and die. Pray to Wakan Tanka for power, little one. The day will come for you to take up the lance."

Mastincala tried to lift his spirits at that notion, but he couldn't. Dreaming of the good fight was an old man's tonic. Too much despair choked the hearts of the young.

"Ah, it's not anger that makes your heart heavy," the medicine man said, gripping the Rabbit with both hands on shoulders seemingly too small to bear their burden.

"No," Mastincala confessed. "Tacante is dead. Hinhan Hota is gone. I am afraid."

"Afraid?" the old man asked, laughing. "What can a man be afraid of? The winds blow. Clouds bring the thunder. A man lives and dies. Why should he fear what is certain to happen anyway?"

"You're old. Don't you fear death?"

"It's part of the Great Mystery, this dying," He Hopa explained. "When we breathe no more, it seems there is nothing. But after we sleep, don't we wake to rise again? When we close our eyes on this life, we begin the long walk on the other side."

"What's it like there?" Mastincala asked.

"Ah, that is the mystery," He Hopa said solemnly. "But I don't fear what I don't know, little one. Far beyond what I can see, the sacred hoop of life continues. Other people walk other prairies there. Great waters flow into lakes larger than any I will ever see. So it's said. I haven't been there. I don't fear those places, and I don't fear the other side."

Such strong talk helped a heart be brave. It was needed, for the march to Fort Laramie was long and difficult. Sharp rocks cut the bare feet of the people. Hot days and cold nights brought fever and death. The dead were wrapped in their blankets and laid on rock ledges. The soldiers didn't trouble them, for there was great fear of fever.

Mastincala often grew light-headed, but He Hopa bled the elbow, sang a healing song, and painted the scar with healing powders.

"It will heal," the medicine man pronounced, and Mastincala cast aside his own doubts. Pain could be endured. It had been.

Most days the boys saw to the needs of those animals the soldiers allowed now to carry the very weak. There were fires to tend, too. The women and girls saw to the cooking, as was the custom. But there was no hunting or fishing or warrior games. The soldiers wouldn't permit it.

Mastincala looked forward to trail's end. There was talk among the people that the great white father might punish Harney for killing Little Thunder's people. Seven dozens were slain, so it was said. And though the soldiers spoke of a battle, Mastincala knew how many of the dead had been helpless—women and little ones. Some soldiers knew the truth. They were certain to speak it.

But when Harney's soldiers arrived at the little fort, they spoke only of the lesson they had delivered to the Sioux murderers. Sioux! These wasicuns knew so little they called the people by a Frenchman's word.

Mastincala bowed his head in shame as he and the other captives were paraded like ponies before the people of a wagon train. The wasicun mothers pointed fingers while their children spit ugly words. The men kept their rifles close by, afraid that a tired, near naked band of Lakota women and little ones would strike out at their tormentors.

Then Mastincala heard his name called. From ahead a small, dark-haired boy appeared. He wore the brown cloth trousers of the wasicun, but his shirt was of buckskin. His eyes filled with anger and sadness as they gazed upon the scarecrow features of a friend.

Your blood is mostly wasicun, Hinkpila, Mastincala thought as young Louis Le Doux broke past the soldiers and raced to embrace his friend. *But your heart is with the Lakota people,* the Rabbit observed as he collapsed with exhaustion. And in what had grown more and more to be a friendless world, Louis's smiling face was the most welcome of sights.

Chapter Four

A thick stew prepared by Charlotte Le Doux, Louis's mother, soon brought Mastincala back to life. The soldiers took little interest in the Lakota children, and so many of them escaped the privations of the captive camp. Post traders took some in. Others were soon accepted into other quarters. For the destruction of Little Thunder's camp did not pass unnoticed by the Lakota people. Soon an Oglala band appeared on the Platte. Among the warriors who rode to the fort was Hinhan Hota, the Gray Owl.

Mastincala's heart soared at the sight of the broad-shouldered Owl. The captive camp soon warmed with the knowledge that others thought dead were among those who had remained in the camp. Few smiled at the soldiers encamped beyond the fort buildings, though. Each sad-faced child seemed to remind its elders of the eighty-six slain.

Hinhan Hota and the others left their horses to drink at the banks of the Laramie River. They strode toward the fort with stern faces, carrying rifles, and clearly angry that so many remained encircled by the soldier camp. Mastincala wanted to rush to the men, tell of what he had seen and survived, but Louis's father, the trader René Le Doux, held the boy back.

"I will go," Le Doux announced. "Louis, you must stay here. There may be trouble, like when the soldiers marched on Conquering Bear's camp."

Louis quickly translated, and Mastincala drew back. The thought of another fight, and the loss of a second father, was more than a boy of seven could bear.

In the end, there was no fight. Colonel Harney warned the Oglalas and their brother Sicangus that the army would punish the Lakotas again should they lift their lances against soldiers.

"Ah, nothing good will come of this," Le Doux said afterward. "He treats warriors like children, and he insists on taking hostages to assure the peace."

Indeed, several young men offered themselves to the soldiers in return for the release of their relatives. It pained Mastincala to watch such fine young warriors shackled and led off to the iron-box lodge. It was said the soldiers would take the hostages far away and punish them hard for the bad deeds of their people. Even those whose blood had begun to cool had bad hearts for the wasicuns afterward.

For Mastincala, though, it was a good time. Hinhan Hota wasted no time inviting Tasiyagnunpa to his lodge. It was not unusual for a man to adopt his slain brother's family, or to wed a widowed wife. Hinhan Hota took little Wicatankala for his own, and Mastincala was soon as much a son as one born to the Owl's loins could have been.

The Oglala camp moved along as autumn approached, but Hinhan Hota kept his lodge near the fort. He, like Tacante, had been born to the Oglala band, but his new wife was Sicangu. Other Oglala warriors, some with wives and some without, chose also to adopt the fatherless among Little Thunder's camp. He Hopa, the medicine man, remained as well, and many looked to the wisdom of Four Horns for direction.

"A younger man must lead the people," He Hopa insisted. And so it came about that Hinhan Hota became chief of the band.

Mastincala swelled with pride when he learned his father was so honored. He also felt the heavy weight of responsibility that fell upon the shoulders of a chief's son. Many eyes would follow his steps along the sacred path, and he worried he would never be tall or strong as the Owl.

"You will grow," Louis argued when the two boys spoke of it while fishing the Platte. "As I will. He Hopa says the wakan comes to us often as a trickster, and we must not let our power turn us to the bad faces, the angry ones."

Mastincala agreed. And as the moon rose and fell, he began finally to grow. No Lakota would mistake him for the giant spruce or pine, but few taunted him as the little Rabbit now. Capa was dead and the other boys stared at the scarred elbow and nodded knowingly. Mastincala, rabbit boy, had been the one to return to the burning camp. He had stood at his dead father's side. On Rabbit's face the wasicuns had read no fear.

Hinhan Hota was a quiet leader. From him came no stirring call to battle, no tall boasts. He led, and those who chose to follow did so. But his example as a hunter and bringer of ponies increased his following. The Owl raided the Crows on Powder River and swept the Pawnees south of the North Platte. And as the people journeyed across the prairie and into the hills on the sacred hoop journey foretold in the heavens overhead, he brought new hope and power to the Sicangus.

Mastincala learned many lessons from Hinhan Hota. The boy could soon recognize the fastest among a pony herd, and his strong legs and small stature made him the fleetest among his fellows. Only Hinkpila could match his pace, and the trader's son stayed mostly in the shadow of the fort.

Louis was also a teacher. Even as the Rabbit taught his friend new Lakota words, so Short Hair passed along English phrases to the young Sicangu. Louis had two brothers and a sister, and his father was glad to let the half-wild colt run with the Lakota, the people of Louis's grandmother. Hinhan Hota didn't mind. He recognized better than most the hole left in a man's heart who had no brother.

"Soon you will have a brother of your own blood," the Owl told Mastincala one night, pointing to Tasiyagnunpa's swelling belly.

The Rabbit stood as tall as a smallish boy could in his tenth summer and howled his joy. Then he turned to Louis.

"I have a brother already, Ate," Mastincala declared a moment later.

"Ah, Hinkpila, you are always welcome to my fire," Hinhan Hota spoke. "My lodge is your home. We have many Crow ponies and much wasna. We will call the people together and invite you into our family. Tomorrow we feast and make many presents. He Hopa will prepare the pipe. Mastincala will be your brother, and I will be your father. Hau, my sons!"

"Hau!" Mastincala echoed. Louis howled even louder.

The making of a relative was not undertaken lightly among the Lakota people. Even as the people gathered, old He Hopa, the medicine man, set about preparing for the ritual. First sweet grass was spread on four coals to entice good influences. Then tobacco was offered to the four directions, to Wakan Tanka, the all-knowing mystery, and to Mother Earth. He Hopa prayed to each in turn.

He Hopa brought forth Louis, the light-skinned boy, and spoke of the ancient rite of Hunkapi, the making of relatives. Once, long before, the Rees had come to the Lakota people in search of sacred corn taken by a Lakota holy man. The holy man, known as Bear Boy, was given the rite of peacemaking in a vision. Now the same ceremony brought a bonding of bands, of tribes, or even joined a boy to a family.

Before the time of trouble, He Hopa recounted, men without sons often took into their lodge a boy from a large or poor family. In such a way a promising youth was allied to a strong man while not losing his blood relations, either. Such an event was always marked with feasting and a giveaway.

After He Hopa conducted the rite, Mastincala proclaimed gifts of Crow ponies to three young men from poor families. The giving was in honor of his new brother, though the gifts went to those in greater need. The ponies being of great value, Louis Le Doux became in the eyes of the band a young man of worth.

All ate well that night, and the great stocks of wasna shrank considerably. As a result, Hinhan Hota chose to take the new brothers on a hunt. The boys could scarcely conceal their excitement, for going to the hunt with a chief was an honor at any time. For boys so young, it hinted of promise.

Mastincala had his doubts. He carried a light bow with which he had killed small game. Louis had often taken a turn at the bow, but the Owl ordered it left behind. Two frowns answered the command, and disappointment flooded the boys' faces.

"I hunt brother elk," Hinhan Hota explained. "Your arrows would never pierce his tough hide. For such an undertaking, a man must carry the warrior's bow."

Gray Owl then produced a wondrous bow of soft ash, carved with great affection for a treasured son by a loving father. The grip was wrapped in buffalo hide with strips of beadwork on each side.

"Wicatankala," the chief explained as he traced the beadwork. The pattern resembled a rabbit running. So that was what Gull had devoted her evenings to!

"Ate, it is a wonder," Mastincala declared. "But my arm is still short."

"For this bow it is a strong heart that's needed," Hinhan Hota answered. "String it, my son."

Rabbit bent the bow and drew the string taut. He then raised it triumphantly.

"And Hinkpila?" Mastincala asked.

"Ah, I had time to make the one bow only," Hinhan Hota explained. "Perhaps brothers can share?"

"Hau!" they cried together.

The three of them then gathered such belongings as might be needed and walked to the pony herd. The Owl selected three spry ponies and ordered the boys to place their bone saddles atop the animals. Hinhan Hota did likewise. He then tied his rifle behind him and led the way toward a distant hillside. The boys followed in silence.

By late afternoon Gray Owl had selected a likely spot, a clearing just above a small pond. He then secured his horse, assured himself the boys had done the same, and led the way through dense underbrush toward the edge of the clearing. Mastincala took note of how the wind stung his eyes. The Owl had brought them downwind so the elk wouldn't sniff their scent on the breeze.

"Now we must make prayers," Hinhan Hota explained. He invoked Wakan Tanka to reward their devotion with fresh meat, and he offered the customary tobacco. Afterward the three hunters spread out patiently on the edge of the meadow and waited.

Mastincala notched an arrow, but his fingers grew stiff and numb before he had occasion to draw back his bowstring. Louis had more patience. But Hinhan Hota seemed carved of stone. The chief watched with steady eyes as rabbits hurried by. Quail sang in a nearby thicket. Mastincala chewed a strip of buffalo hide and hoped the elk would come before his hair was white with age like He Hopa's.

"Each thing in its time," Hinhan Hota had so often reminded his son. Well, elk tracks marked the pond as a favorite drinking spot. They said nothing of when or how often!

Finally the elk appeared. There were five in all, and the Owl motioned toward a buck on the far right side. It was neither the eldest nor the youngest. Mastincala motioned that he understood. Then the boy drew back the string, held the bow steady, and took aim. He let fly the arrow, and it struck the elk in the throat. Hinhan Hota fired the instant the first elk collapsed.

"He's not dead," Louis observed, pointing to how the first animal struggled to breathe as blood dripped down its neck. Mastincala handed over the bow, and Louis fired a second arrow through the elk's stout heart. The animal died instantly.

The other elk had by now scattered, but two elk would provide what meat was needed. Hinhan Hota then suggested the hides would make fine winter coats, and Louis appeared especially pleased. An elk robe would mark him as a man to know among the wasicuns at the fort.

Skinning the animals and packing the meat occupied the hunters until early dusk. The boys rode back to camp on the same horse. The other dragged a travois behind it with the meat. Mastincala noticed his father's proud gaze, and when the three of them entered the camp together, they were met with shouts and brave heart calls.

"Hau, Mastincala! Rabbit has killed an elk!" the other boys exclaimed. "Hau, Hinkpila! Short Hair is blooded!"

Mastincala gazed down at his fellows from the top of his horse and grinned. For once he was the tall one. Perhaps it was a brave heart that mattered most after all. He hoped so, for he enjoyed the good feeling.

It was well that Hinhan Hota and the boys had killed the elk, for winter came early. In a fortnight, snows had packed the ground, and even the elk's tough hide couldn't fend off the bite of the frigid north wind. It was in this time of cold that Tasiyagnunpa went to the women's lodge to give birth.

The Owl saw to it an old woman came to tend the lodge, for Wablosa had been killed at Ash Hollow. She was called Yellow Cow, and Mastincala judged her skin as hard and wrinkled as an old moccasin. Her tongue was sharp as a killing lance, though, and she enjoyed flaying her male charges with rawhide thongs. Gray Owl had left to pray for an easy birth, so Rabbit and Louis left Wicatankala to the care of Yellow Cow and sought the lodge of He Hopa.

The medicine man welcomed the visit. Winter brought the old man pain, for his brittle fingers swelled, and his legs were bent by too many battle wounds. He had a pair of young women to cook and care for him, but he mostly grumbled at their slowness or complained they grew fat on his wasna.

"It's well you've come, Mastincala," He Hopa declared as he huddled with the youngsters around a fire. "There is death on the wind. Your mother hurries a child into the world?"

"Han," Rabbit answered. Yes. Of course, He Hopa knew she was in the women's lodge. Four Horns, after all, had been the one to urge prayers on Gray Owl.

"It's bad your brother chooses this time to be born," He Hopa said soberly. "Winter is a time for things to die. The leaves fall from the trees, and the prairie grasses grow yellow. Bear takes to his den. He is the only wise one."

Mastincala agreed, and Louis nodded.

"I've had brothers born before, but always their eyes closed too soon for me to whisper their names," Mastincala said sadly. "Ate says hard times are before us, for the wasicun has a bad face for the Lakota. We will need warriors. Hinhan Hota needs a son."

Louis nodded again, and He Hopa rose. He flung off the blanket he'd drawn tight against his shoulders, then began chanting. Each word he muttered with gritted teeth as the chill ate its way into his ancient, emaciated body. Then Mastincala looked on in disbelief as the medicine man stripped off his buckskins, leaving him naked save for a breechclout. The boys eyed each other gravely. Then Mastincala discarded his elk robe and likewise stripped off his outer clothing. Louis did the same, and the three of them danced about the fire, shivering with cold and singing an ancient song.

"Hear me, Wakan Tanka," He Hopa began. "We are ashes to your fire, consumed in an instant. Grant us power that our song may make the little one strong. Give him a brave heart. Send sun to warm his bones and make the blood flow quick."

He Hopa then drew a knife and made twin cuts across his chest. Blood trickled from the wounds, and Mastincala stared in wonder at how the old medicine man cried even louder and danced with new vigor.

"Hear me, Wakan Tanka," the Rabbit called as he drew his own knife and held the blade against his chest. Cold steel touched the bare flesh, but Mastincala couldn't bring his fingers to press the blade.

"Have brave hearts," He Hopa urged.

Louis drew his knife then, and Mastincala took a deep breath. He wouldn't allow his new brother to make the sacrifice alone. The knife cut shallow red lines in the taut flesh, and Mastincala fought the need to cry out. Twinges of pain brought a spasm of energy to him, and he danced as a wild man. The feel of the warm blood running down his belly startled his senses. He gazed over at Louis and noticed how much brighter the blood seemed when dripping down the nutmeg-colored flesh of his companion.

"Ay, hah, hah," He Hopa chanted. "Wakan Tanka, hear our prayer."

And so, on they danced until exhaustion overcame them. Louis collapsed first. Then Mastincala dropped to his knees. He Hopa, who was white-haired the day both were born, continued on until a crier brought word a boy was born to Hinhan Hota.

"Dress yourselves, young ones," He Hopa told his freezing disciples. "You have a brother."

"Hau!" Mastincala bellowed. "A brother!"

Louis grinned his agreement as he hurried to pull a shirt over his bare ribs. The boys had little luck with their clothes, and finally He Hopa motioned for his women to help. The girls giggled and clucked like old hens as they warmed the youngsters. He Hopa then threw buffalo hides beside the fire and wrapped the boys like cocoons.

Mastincala awoke the next morning still enclosed in his hide. Louis was warming his stiff joints beside the fire. Outside the sun had broken through a heavy haze, and melting snow dripped from the heavy hides covering the tipi.

"I have a brother?" Mastincala asked.

"Eat this," He Hopa said, shoving a flat corn cake into the Rabbit's mouth. "There is tea there. Drink it. Your father waits."

Louis laughed to see Mastincala in such a hurry. Moments later the two boys stumbled out into the snowdrifts together. When they reached Hinhan Hota's lodge, the chief clasped them both by the shoulders.

"Welcome your brother," Gray Owl called, motioning toward the bundle of fur clasped in old Yellow Cow's arms. The boys stepped closer, and the old woman allowed them a single glimpse of the wrinkled brown face beneath.

"He's called Itunkala," their sister explained.

"A good name," Tasiyagnunpa announced. Still weak and weary, she lay in buffalo hides beside the fire.

A good name? Mastincala asked himself. It meant Mouse. If there was a name sure to grant its owner a steeper path than Rabbit, Mouse was certain to be it.

"He will need a brave heart and a strong arm," Mastincala declared.

"And a brother to show him the way," Hinhan Hota added.

"Such a brother he will have," Mastincala promised. Louis clasped his brother's wrist. A smile emerged on the paler boy's lips. Rabbit guiding Mouse? Yes, it was worth a laugh surely.

"I have a young brother already," Louis whispered. "The Lakota call him Istamaza."

"Istamaza?" Mastincala asked. Eyeglasses?

"He doesn't see well," Louis explained. "The soldier doctor made him some spectacles. It would be worse if his skin wasn't so light. His hair is fair, too, like yellow grass. He will be a better white man."

"You are Lakota now," Mastincala declared. "You will stay here with me. We will ride to the buffalo hunt and fight the Crows."

"No, my father will come soon, and I will return to the fort," Louis muttered. "I, too, have a hard road to walk, it seems."

"The road of the wasicun?" Mastincala asked. "That is a crazy trail!"

"So it must seem," Louis confessed with a grin. "I'll come back, though, and we'll hunt again."

"Yes," Mastincala agreed. "Many buffalo will fall to our arrows."

Chapter Five

Louis's departure a few days later left Mastincala cold and hollow. Difficult days were at hand, and he now felt he faced them alone. There was a winter as bitter cold and frozen as any remembered by the old ones. Chills gripped the small and the helpless, and Mastincala worried over the survival of his small brother. But Wakan Tanka willed the child would survive, and ice, as always, thawed under the dancing suns of summer.

As Mastincala prepared to meet the challenges of his twelfth summer, great changes shook the earth. Word came that war had broken out among the white men in the country beyond the great waters.

"Ah, they are a quarrelsome people," He Hopa declared. "It is like them to fight among themselves."

When Louis arrived to share the buffalo hunt, he told of great armies of graycoats who fought the bluecoat soldier chiefs. A hundred times a hundred were slain, it was said. Mastincala shook his head in doubt. How could so many people be killed? Even the wasicun thunder guns could not bring such a calamity to pass.

"It's so," Louis insisted, and He Hopa reminded the Rabbit how the eagle chief Harney had made war upon the peaceful camp of the Sicangu at Blue Creek.

"Then perhaps all the wasicuns will die," Mastincala said. "Then the Lakota people can live in the old way, walking the sacred road, with only the Crows and Snakes to fight."

As snows came again to the plain, thawed, and faded under the golden glow of the summer sun, it seemed perhaps it would be just so. The wagon trains that rolled along Platte River grew fewer, and mostly now it seemed there were women and little ones together with old men on that road. Few soldiers kept watch on the wasicun forts. At Laramie only the old and lame occupied the long lodges.

For Mastincala, those two years were a remembered time. He hunted and fished and grew taller. His shoulders broadened, and his voice deepened. While bathing in the chill streams of Paha Sapa, he saw that he was a boy no longer. Next day Hinhan Hota drew him aside.

"Each Lakota is called in his own hour to be a man, my son," the Owl explained. "This is your time. No one among the people could have stood so tall in his boyhood. All that must now be forgotten. You go to walk the warrior path. Hau, it makes a father's heart sing!"

Hinhan Hota then led Mastincala to the lodge of He Hopa. The old medicine man was waiting, his eager eyes betraying his feelings.

"So, you are a boy no more, Rabbit," He Hopa said. "Much waits to be done. Much. You are ready?"

"I am ready," the young man replied solemnly.

"Then it is well we should begin."

Mastincala followed He Hopa inside the lodge. The young man then sat beside the elder and listened to admonitions concerning the responsibilities of a Lakota. There was lore to be passed along, stories of boldness and daring. Finally, when He Hopa was satisfied all was in order, he escorted Mastincala out of the tipi.

"It's time for him to seek his vision," He Hopa announced.

Hinhan Hota then appeared. The Owl led his son to the edge of the camp before halting. Wicatankala arrived carrying a fine cloth breechclout and a pair of beaded moccasins.

"These are for my brother," she said, never looking directly at Mastincala. "They will bring him a brave heart in his search for a dream."

Mastincala accepted the fine moccasins and the breechclout with a silent nod. Wicatankala then left. Her role was over, for the rite that followed, the seeking of a vision, was also a boy's introduction into Lakota manhood. It was as ancient as the Lakota people, and in all that time fathers had introduced their sons to the wakan, the mystery, of the rite.

Hinhan Hota took great care to strip Mastincala of his boyhood clothes. Though the air was cold and the wind sharp, he was given only the new breechclout and the moccasins to wear.

"Today is the beginning of manhood," the Owl explained. "I peel away all that is false and send you naked before Wakan Tanka. Open your heart to the great mystery that is life, my son."

Hinhan Hota then conducted Mastincala to a rocky cliff some distance from the camp. There he was instructed to remain until he received a vision.

"You may pray and sing, Mastincala," his father explained. "But no food or drink may pass your lips. The starving shows you are worthy of the dream. When it comes, pay great heed to it. All that follows in your time as a man will flow from this dream."

Hinhan Hota then left the Rabbit alone in the rocks. For a time Mastincala stood in the sharp breeze, confused, wondering how one might bring on a vision. The silence haunted him. He felt cut off from his family, from his band, from all he knew. And as he stood in that lonely place, the hunger began to gnaw at his belly.

"Hear me, Wakan Tanka," Mastincala finally prayed. "Bring to my heart the knowledge I seek. Show me the sacred road I must walk."

He then sang a brave heart song. Afterward he prayed again.

Never did the sun cross the heavens so slowly. Day lasted a lifetime, it seemed. And when darkness arrived, Mastincala faced it with the same chant and the same prayer. His throat was parched, and his belly ached with want. Still he refused to cry out. He shivered with cold that night, then blinked his eyes as a bright sun tormented him the next morning. Hau! Manhood was not as easily faced as he imagined. And as he suffered, he wondered what became of a boy denied a vision. There was but a single answer. He died of hunger or exhaustion.

Toward dusk his voice grew weak. His tongue swelled, and sweat left his body weak with fatigue. Finally he could stand no longer. His knees buckled, and he fell.

Then the dream came.

It was unlike anything he had seen or felt before. His soul seemed to be floating on a cloud. He was swept along on the wind over a broad plain, past familiar hills and mountains, above rivers and streams where he had swum and fished. He saw bands of Crows and Snakes, war parties of Pawnees, buckskinned wasicuns with their hairy faces and flintlock rifles. Finally he descended to the plain.

Now he was Tatanka, Bull Buffalo, rumbling over the yellow grass prairie, leading the humped multitude on the run. Thunder exploded behind him, and great yellow blades of lightning split the gray heavens.

"I am Tatanka," a deep, sorrowful voice seemed to boom across the world. "See how my power shakes all the earth! Who will sing the brave heart song and follow me?"

Mastincala wanted to boast that he, the Rabbit, would follow, but only that booming voice emerged from his lips. It was no longer for him to follow as a boy might. Now he must lead!

The dream took him many places, for Tatanka seemed able to follow the Lakota star map painted upon the sky. He marched across the plains to Pe Sla, the sacred hoop, then rumbled on to Mato Tipila, the Bear's Lodge mountain to the west. When Bull Buffalo had finally completed his journey, he stopped. Where before a thundering herd had followed, now there were but a few.

"Hau, my way is sacred," Tatanka said. "The road is hard, and few feet can stay upon it. Hau, have the brave heart! Come, follow me."

Again Mastincala wanted to answer, but the words were his own. He swelled with pride, for the call to lead would bring honor. Then he felt himself floating again, drifting upon a cloud. Overwhelming darkness swallowed him, and there was only the numbing cold of the night to torment his bare flesh.

Hinhan Hota brought him down from his solitude the next morning. Mastincala was weak and could hardly stand. The first droplets of water that touched his lips brought forth a fierce thirst, and he hungered for the taste of wasna. He got neither. Instead, he was conducted to a water hole.

"Ate, my dream," Mastincala muttered.

"Hold it close to your heart, my son," Hinhan Hota urged. "Soon you must tell He Hopa. The old one will help you to see its meaning."

Mastincala nodded, then surrendered his will to the Owl.

Sunka Sapa, the Black Dog, and Waawanyanka, the Watcher, now arrived to help restore Mastincala to the living. The two young men were but a summer older than the Rabbit, and both were eager to provide assistance to a young man with no older brothers or cousins. Hinhan Hota oversaw a careful washing, for Mastincala must cleanse himself of all that had come before. Then he was fed enough to restore his senses. Finally Hinhan Hota escorted his son to the medicine lodge. He Hopa was waiting.

"We must bring back the dreaming," the medicine man explained as he helped the Rabbit inside the nearby tipi. "You remember?"

"Yes," Mastincala said, forcing his eyes to focus on the wrinkled old man.

"Tell it all," He Hopa urged, and Mastincala then related the strange dream.

He Hopa had sat quietly as Mastincala recounted the dream. Even when the young man finished, He Hopa remained stone-faced, silent.

"What does it mean?" the Rabbit asked. "Am I to be a leader among our people?"

"Perhaps," Four Horns said, gazing at Mastincala's forehead. "That is not for you and I to say. If a man sets out upon a path, others may follow."

"What path?"

"Tatanka calls to your heart. Bull Buffalo is sacred among all the creatures that walk the earth. It is he who gives us the warm coats and coverings for our lodges. He fills our bellies in the cold moons of winter. He is beloved to Wakan Tanka. A man who follows Tatanka would give himself to the people, seeking only their good, even as Tacante, the man who was your father, did."

"I am to sacrifice myself then," Mastincala said, digesting the news somberly.

"It's a hard road, little friend. It will take a brave heart. This you have."

"Yes," Mastincala said, stiffening his shoulders.

"Tatanka promises great power to the man who walks his path. He will need it, for there is great peril."

"Tacante told me you promised him a short life if he put on the people's shirt, agreeing to tend their needs. Is my walk also to be a short one?"

"Nothing in the dream speaks of this," He Hopa explained.

"But you have great power to see what will come."

"Not so great as to say how long a man should live," He Hopa explained. "I have told you it is a hard path Tatanka calls you to walk. But Wakan Tanka watches the brave hearts. So you will be watched, nephew."

He Hopa stood and walked to the far side of the lodge. He rummaged among his belongings until he located a pouch made from a bull buffalo's bladder. The bag was decorated with elk teeth and hair, and a sacred red rock dangled from a rawhide thong on one side.

"This is strong medicine, Mastincala," He Hopa declared. "So long as you remain true to Tatanka, so it will keep you safe. Hau, it holds great power!"

"Thank you, He Hopa," Mastincala said, accepting the gift.

"I now walk the bent backbone days of my life," the old man said, clutching his young companion's wrists. "Soon my time upon the earth will be at an end. Give me your eyes and ears, young one, that I can teach you the mysteries of the wakan, the sacred ways."

"But I am to be a warrior."

"A warrior has need of medicine, too, Mastincala," He Hopa said gravely. "More so if he is to lead. There are great dangers in the world to come, and a man who can see them will save the people from great harm."

"I will learn all I can," Mastincala promised.

"Hau!" the old man then shouted as he led Mastincala from the lodge. "Look here, my brothers, and see Mastincala reborn as a man."

"Hau!" Hinhan Hota cried, and the shout was taken up by others among the camp. Hokala, the Badger, who had so often tormented Mastincala the boy, yelled loudest of all, for he had only just completed his own dreaming. Cehupa Maza, the Iron Jaw, clasped Mastincala by the shoulders, as did others.

"My son is a man," Hinhan Hota declared proudly as he presented Mastincala to his young brother, Itunkala. The Mouse climbed up into Mastincala's arms. Tasiyagnunpa and Wicatankala gazed with admiration upon the new man among their people.

Mastincala noticed great differences in the way he was now treated. Women retreated at his approach, and young maidens often gazed shyly as he passed nearby or else giggled among themselves. He rode to the buffalo hunt with the warriors, and he was expected to supply game for the kettle.

At first he felt cut off. His mother and sister were occupied with Itunkala, the small one. Nothing was expected of the child. Mastincala grew envious, especially when the long days riding the buffalo valleys left him weary and lonely.

"A warrior rides alone upon his horse," Sunka Sapa lamented as the two young men topped a ridge, only to see there was nothing but another ridge beyond. "Hau! Who will sing the scalp song when I fight my enemies? Only a sister."

But there were times when a boy of fourteen would choose no other fate than to ride as a Lakota warrior. Three days after slaying two buffalo cows and rescuing a dismounted Sunka Sapa from a charging bull, Mastincala was brought before his family.

"Here is my warrior son," Hinhan Hota boasted. The Owl then offered Mastincala a fine shield made of hump hide from a bull buffalo. From it hung tufts of hair given with prayers to keep its holder safe. The face of the shield bore the countenance of Tatanka, the Bull Buffalo, surrounded by white clouds torn by lightning streaks.

"Ate, it is a strong shield," Mastincala observed. "I'll carry it proudly, remembering the one who made it."

"Hau!" Hinhan Hota shouted. "Be worthy of it, my son."

So Mastincala swore he would be.

Chapter Six

With the wasicun soldiers busy fighting among themselves in the out-of-sight lands beyond Platte River, the Lakotas enjoyed a time of peace. Oh, there were still raids against the Crows in the north, the Snakes in the western mountains, and the Pawnees south of the Platte, but those fights were little matter. Even the Pawnees, who carried the white man's rifles and fought in his fashion, didn't raid whole villages or cut down women and little ones. Most of the raiders were after horses, though at times women or children were stolen. More often than not, captives were retrieved, and sometimes the horses, too.

There was honor and respect among the fighters, and rarely was killing necessary. Where a warrior could count a coup upon his enemy, with hand or bow or lance, that was done. Only when the blood grew too hot for reason was much killing done. For when a man was killed, surely a brother or son would raise the cry for revenge.

Mastincala had little heart for war. His mind held too many memories of the Blue Creek fight, of his father's death. But near the close of summer, when Mastincala was still a young man of fourteen summers, Cehupa Maza, Iron Jaw, located a Crow camp with many horses on Powder River. Hinhan Hota invited his son along on the planned raid.

"Ah, this will be a remembered time," Hokala, the Badger, boasted.

"I will take many Crow horses. Maybe I will take one of their women."

"It's said the Crow women are fat," Cehupa Maza said. "She will fall upon you, Hokala, and crush you to marrow."

"I will choose a skinny one," Hokala replied. "I will fatten her on elk steaks and buffalo ribs."

"She'll certainly put a knife in your own ribs at the first chance," He Hopa said, joining the circle of young men who were readying themselves for the raid. "Crow women are treacherous. They have no love of the Lakotas. Their men have good guns, too. Here, paint your foreheads with ash from the fire so their eyes will not find you in the dark. Tie an elk's tooth in your hair for luck."

He Hopa provided the charms and even helped the Badger tie his behind one ear. The young men respected the wise one's advice, and they made such prayers as He Hopa deemed helpful.

Their elders then took charge of the raid. Hinhan Hota and a younger warrior known as Wapaha Luta, Red Lance, were foremost among the eight proven warriors. Cehupa Maza, having first spied the camp, went along, as did Mastincala, Hokala, and four other young men. Two boys of twelve rode along to help handle the stolen ponies, but they left their bows behind. With only a knife for a weapon, such small ones wouldn't rush into a fight and spoil the raid.

Mastincala carried his fine ash bow and a full quiver of arrows. He brought along the buffalo shield, too, and he tied a good iron-bladed knife onto his leg. Except for a breechclout and moccasins, he rode naked. He Hopa had painted his light skin red, and he seemed more ghost than Lakota. Mastincala hoped the Crows would find him so.

He rode erect, proudly displaying the feather awarded him for standing before the bear long ago. The lance wore a bonnet full of coup feathers, and many of the men decorated their hair with eagle plumes. Hinhan Hota disdained decorations, for his medicine was only strong when he rode to battle in simple dress. Tasiyagnunpa lamented that her husband could not show off her fine beadwork, but a warrior never went against his medicine and lived. Everyone knew that.

Of the other young men, only Sunka Sapa, Black Dog, dressed with distinction. His mother's father had passed into his hands a bracelet molded of silver, taken from a wasicun trapper who had come into Paha Sapa to hunt and been captured by the Lakotas. It was a beautiful thing, bright as the moon, and Hinhan Hota argued it might attract the eyes of the Crows. The Dog would not be swayed from wearing it, though, for his grandfather had led many successful war parties against the Rees.

"We don't come to this place to kill Crows," Hinhan Hota reminded the party. "We go to take their horses and leave them to walk naked back to their women. Killing will bring them down on us, and there are enough among us who have sung the mourning songs and made the ghost giveaway."

"Hau, these are good words," Wapaha Luta agreed. "Give us brave hearts to make this ride, Wakan Tanka! Let all return."

"Hau!" the others cried wildly. Afterward they rode in silence toward the Crow camp.

Among all the peoples who rode the plain, the Crows were most skilled at stealing horses. They bred the best to create stock prized among all their neighbors. But good as they were at stealing, the Crows now suffered at the hands of Lakota raiders.

Hinhan Hota had struck the Crows twice. Always before, the Crows had awakened to find their horses gone and their pony guards stripped and bound to cottonwoods. The Owl planned a third such success. He approached the Crow camp on a dark, moonless eve, and he spread out his small band so that they avoided the guards and got between the horse herd and the camp.

"Now, brothers, hear me," Hinhan Hota told the six raiders he took under his leadership. "There are only boys watching the horses. I will capture the one by the water. Wapaha Luta will tend the ones on the far side. Then I will raise a howl, and we will drive the horses away."

The assembled raiders whispered their assent. Then the Owl set out after the guard. There was a small splash, followed by the sound of an object colliding with the ground. Mastincala held his breath a moment. Then his father appeared in the faint light, and the Rabbit prepared to drive off the horses. Before Hinhan Hota could give the shout, though, a rifle discharged.

"One of the guards," Hokala cried in alarm.

The Crow camp rose instantly. Warriors raced naked from their beds toward the horse herd. A boy ran by Mastincala, his yellow shirt torn across one shoulder and stained by blood. In moments the well-laid plan was forgotten. The men waved blankets at the Crow ponies and screamed terrifying yells to set the animals to flight. The young men rode along or fought to avoid the stampede.

The Crows had done much trading with the wasicuns, and their many rifles now sent lead balls tearing at the air. One cut a braid of Mastincala's hair and stung his ear.

"Ayyy!" the Rabbit howled in anger as he turned his horse back toward the onrushing Crows. Cehupa Maza was driving the last of the ponies along, and Mastincala's heart raced at the sight. Indeed, Iron Jaw hadn't forgotten their purpose. And even though three Crow rifles fired in his direction, the young Lakota rode along unhurt.

Not so his horse. A ball plunged through the pony's side and stopped its heart. With a terrible shriek, the horse collapsed, pitching Cehupa Maza into a tangled nest of nettle.

"Ayyy!" Mastincala shouted a second time. This time he galloped toward his fallen comrade, extending an arm so that Iron Jaw could draw himself up behind Mastincala atop the horse. A tall Crow charged them both, and Mastincala grabbed his bow, notched an arrow, and fired all in one motion. The arrow struck the Crow in the right hip, and the warrior cried out in pain. Howling a third time, Mastincala then charged toward the fallen Crow. He slapped the enemy across his chest with the fine ash bow, then turned again and fled toward the other Lakotas and the thundering herd of Crow ponies.

"You counted coup!" Iron Jaw exclaimed as they thundered on. "And rescued me also. Two brave deeds! Hau, you are a great man this day, Mastincala!"

So others thought as well. When the raiders returned with their eighty captured ponies, prayers of thankfulness were made. Then a fire was kindled, and brave deeds were recounted. Red Lance had counted coup on the two Crow boys at the fire, and Hinhan Hota had struck the third. It was the news of Mastincala and his rescue which raised the greatest clamor, though, and when the Rabbit told of his coup upon the Crow, the warriors rose as one.

"Hau! He is surely called by Tatanka to tend his people," He Hopa said as he tied a second and a third feather in Mastincala's hair. "From this time he is Rabbit no longer. He has proven a brave heart, and so he will take a brave name."

"Yes," Hinhan Hota agreed. "I, his father, so give him this name, carried by my own father and given later to my brother. From this day he is known as Tacante."

"Hau!" the warriors cried. For they all knew here was a young man called by Tatanka, one who held above all things the heart of the people. It was right he should be called Buffalo Heart.

In honor of the naming, Hinhan Hota gave five of the captured Crow ponies to families in need of horses. The giveaway marked a father's great esteem for a worthy son, and the young man now called Tacante honored his father with a second giving. He presented two fine ponies to He Hopa, for the medicine man's own horses were aging. One had gone lame.

Others then joined in the giveaway, for all of the raiders could now afford to be generous. Even Itunkala would have his own horse now, and young Hokala was wealthy indeed with five ponies of his own.

It was a remembered day for Tacante. It filled his chest with pride to wear his father's name, a good, ancient name among the Sicangu. And as he put behind him the boy's path, filled with wrestling and swimming and idleness, he held few regrets. His was a path full of promise. *Perhaps*, he thought, *I may even come to be a shirt wearer as the other Tacante was, or even a headman like Hinhan Hota.*

Winter passed into summer, became winter, and passed into summer again, and in that time Tacante did nothing to dim the hopes placed upon him by Hinhan Hota and He Hopa. The young warrior devoted himself to the hunt, and he never rested so long as any among the band were hungry.

He Hopa tutored him in the healing ways, and Tacante grew to know the plants and roots of Paha Sapa and Powder River and the distant snow-crowned peaks of the hecinskayapi, the big-horned sheep. It was into that country that Hinhan Hota led his band the summer of Tacante's sixteenth year.

Tacante himself was disappointed, for Hinkpila, his true friend and adopted brother, had promised to join the buffalo hunt that summer. The wasicuns marked that year, 1864, on their counting papers, and René Le Doux passed along grave news at Fort Laramie.

"The whites are nearly finished with their fighting," Le Doux explained. "The Platte River road is thick with wagons once more, and gold has been found on the Yellowstone. Already wagons cut through the Big Horns on Mr. Bozeman's road. Some are sent back, but others go through. There's been folks killed, and the soldiers talk of building forts."

"That is our country!" Hinhan Hota barked. "Ours promised for all time by the white fathers. We will not give it up."

So others said as well. Among the Oglalas, Mahpiya Luta, Red Cloud, was already protecting the land against the wagon people and the hunters who came to dig the yellow powder from the streams. But it was sure to be a hard fight. Tacante gazed into the faces of the soldiers at the fort. No longer were they old and weary. None walked with the limp. These were young men, and there were many of them. They often rode with the wagon trains.

"It's a bad time to be a Lakota," He Hopa declared. "I have seen a blue cloud swallowing the earth in a dream."

There was fierce talk within the camp, for some had heard of the war fought by Little Crow's Dakotas against the whites in Minnesota. Much death and suffering had befallen those people, and now the Santees were prisoners fenced in on a reservation like the Omahas. A few had come out to join their Lakota brothers, but many were farmers and didn't know the buffalo hunt.

"We are warriors, used to the hard life," Wapaha Luta spoke. "I've fought the white man before. I wear a war bonnet filled with feathers marking the coups I've counted. I go to ride with Red Cloud and the Oglalas."

Others argued against it.

"There are more wasicuns than stars in the sky," said Sinte Gleska, who had been in the white man's jail in Kansas. "We can't kill them all."

"Better to die as a free man than live in a cage," the Lance muttered.

"And what of the women, the little ones?" Hinhan Hota asked. "Will they die as at Blue Creek?"

"Can they live in a cage?" Wapaha Luta asked.

And so the band dissolved. Some families stayed close to the fort, trusting in the treaties. Many others set off west to hunt the buffalo or to join Red Cloud. Tacante was old enough to choose his own path, but he remained with the Owl and old He Hopa. There was Itunkala, after all. And He Hopa hadn't passed along everything he knew.

"What will we do, Ate?" Tacante asked as another three lodges left the fort.

"I have thought long of the choices," Hinhan Hota answered. "There are so few of us left. Mostly young men not proven in battle, with many little ones and old mothers to feed. They should stay, but if I go to Powder River, they will follow."

"Tacante, who was my father, said it is a hard road, leading the people."

"Yes, my son. But when a thing is hard, then it is sure to be right. Wakan Tanka never sends us an easy road, for it would make us weak."

"We go to Powder River, then?"

"It is all I know to do. If there's to be a fight with the wasicun soldiers, there will be need of brave hearts and strong arms."

"Yes," Tacante said, grinning at his father.

Before leaving the fort, Tacante rode into the nearby hills with Hinkpila, Louis Le Doux, to hunt fresh meat for the journey. The two young men, growing tall in their different ways, still shared a closeness for the land and a devotion to each other. They located deer tracks, and Tacante took the lead. Louis hung back, seemingly surprised at the agility and cunning demonstrated by this new person, the Buffalo Heart. Tacante stealthily approached a pair of deer, then drew an arrow from his quiver, notched it, and killed the first animal in an instant. Louis shot the second with his rifle. The choice of weapons, as much as anything, reminded them of how far their paths had diverged.

"You go to Powder River to fight the whites," Louis said as he began butchering his deer. "I'm mostly white myself, Tacante. Oh, the white men don't say it, but I am."

"And I am Lakota," Tacante answered.

"I'm Hinhan Hota's son, too. Your brother. Maybe I, too, should come to Powder River."

"You would be welcome," Tacante said without hesitation. Then he frowned. "But for you, Hinkpila, the white man's road is not so crazy. You wear wasicun clothes and shoot his rifle. If a fight comes, it will be hard on your father for you to be away. You have young brothers and sisters."

"You understand then?"

"There is a word among my people," Tacante said, gripping his friend by the hand. "Kola."

"It means friend."

"More, sometimes. Warriors who have no brother often call each other kola, brother-friend. They share all they have, and their hearts are like one."

"We did this long ago, when you were but a rabbit boy and not a Lakota warrior."

"Yes," Tacante agreed. "I call you kola, Hinkpila."

"And I you, my brother," Louis said, grimly forcing a smile onto his face. "We'll meet again, you know, in a better time."

"Hau! We'll hunt the buffalo then!"

They went on with the butchering, but neither entirely believed there would be another time, or a better one. The paths were so far apart already.

And yet all the world lies within the sacred hoop, Tacante told himself. Don't all paths turn?

Chapter Seven

So it was that Tacante followed Hinhan Hota into the land of the hecin-skayapi. As he rode along atop a tall buckskin pony, he observed the deep ruts cut by wasicun wagons in the Platte River road. The grass there was eaten down to its roots, and there wasn't a hint of the buffalo or antelope which had once frequented the area.

Tacante read his frowning father's thoughts. This was how the wasicuns would paint the Big Horn country! Only there, along Powder River and in the mountains beyond, could the Lakota hunt in the old ways. Once the game was gone, as on Platte River, the people would have to go to the white man's reservations—or starve. Either way, it promised to be a slow death.

Such a vision of the future spurred on Hinhan Hota's small band. They swept across the arid flats beyond the Platte and swung north into the rocky hills which led to Powder River. The young men rode ahead, locating small herds of buffalo or antelope to hunt. It wasn't long, though, before they saw evidence of the passage of wasicuns. Wagon ruts muddied streams, and half-devoured carcasses of elk often spoiled the land.

Yes, Tacante thought. *The wasicun is a crazy man. He sets his feet upon a path, and he continues to walk blindly onward, taking what he wants and killing as he feels the urge. He cut the buffalo valleys with his roads, killed off the game, brought on the spotted sickness to kill the people. Still he wasn't content. He now set his hungry eyes on Powder River, on the hecinskayapi country. It must stop!*

Tacante wasn't the only one to view the rutted intrusion with angry eyes. All his people silently shared that rage. And when Hokala discovered a party of wasicuns camped beside the trail, a dozen voices rose in a call for war.

"This is no time to let the blood talk," He Hopa scolded. "We have long been at peace in this country. I have touched the pen to a paper saying the Lakotas will hold this country always, with no roads to chase away the game or bring forts. These greedy wasicuns are like children. They must be showed the way back, not struck down like a crazed dog."

"The treaty says they will not come here," Cehupa Maza complained. "But the wasicuns don't care. They killed my mother and my sister at Blue Creek, when we were also at peace. They speak of peace, but they make war anyway."

There were many who howled their agreement with young Iron Jaw. Hinhan Hota was not among them.

"We'll meet with these wasicuns," the Owl said. "We'll tell them to go home, that they're not welcome here. If they go, then we won't hinder them. If they continue, we'll punish them."

"Han," the warriors all agreed. Yes, it was a good plan.

And so, after smoking the pipe and invoking Wakan Tanka's aid, Hinhan Hota led Tacante and some of the young men to the camp of the wasicuns.

It wasn't much of a camp. Many times Tacante had seen wagon camps on Platte River with a hundred people. This wasicun band had only two wagons, and most of the men rode mules. Two women were with them, and seven children.

"He Hopa was right," Hinhan Hota declared, pointing at the camp. Here, after all, were men so foolish as to leave their animals to graze unhobbled, without guards. Yes, they were children, needing to be taught.

The Owl spread out his companions so as to encircle the camp. Then he called to the wasicuns.

Instantly the camp came alive. The women collected their little ones and huddled beside the wagons. The men formed a line beside the river. Tacante counted seven, although two of them were no more than boys. All held rifles.

Hinhan Hota called again, but the wasicuns knew nothing of the Lakota words the Owl hurled at them. Hinhan Hota then waved Tacante to his side, and the young warrior translated his father's challenge.

"You shouldn't be here!" Tacante cried. "This is Lakota land by treaty. Go back to Platte River."

"I been this way before!" a tall, hairy-faced wasicun called. "John Bozeman made himself a road through here to the Montana goldfields. You know gold, eh, Injun? We ain't goin' no place 'cept on."

Tacante translated the words for his father and the others. The chief scowled, and Hokala offered to lead the first charge.

"They have many guns," Hinhan Hota pointed out. "They are ready now. We will talk some more. Come, Tacante, we will meet with them."

Tacante trembled slightly as he watched Hinhan Hota dismount. The chief left behind his rifle and bow. Tacante also left his weapons behind. The two of them walked slowly, grimly, toward the wasicuns. Now it was possible to read the fear in the pale faces of the trespassers. Clearly, fighting wasn't in their hearts.

"You must go back now," Tacante translated after his father shouted his demands. "We are many, and you are few. We don't wish to wear your scalps, to kill children and women because they have foolishly gone where they shouldn't."

Hinhan Hota had finished, and he sat before the wasicuns with folded arms. Tacante paused a moment, then added words of his own.

"I know your words," the young warrior explained. "Many days I have spent with wasicuns, with white people. My own brother lives among the traders at Fort Laramie. You know this place? I tell you we don't hunger to close your eyes upon the light. But you can't go on killing the game so that my people will starve. If you turn back and go to Platte River, we won't harm you. If you go on . . ."

Tacante grimly touched the handle of the knife tied to his calf. The wasicuns exchanged worried looks. They could see there were mounted warriors amid the trees on the far ridge and blocking the trail beside the river.

"We wouldn't hurt anybody," the hairy-faced wasicun insisted. "Just mean to go north's all, to the Yellowstone."

"You kill elk that would fill my brother's belly and make him strong," Tacante answered. "You must go back. Or paint your faces for war."

"We'd kill some o' you," a second wasicun argued.

Hinhan Hota asked what the wasicuns spoke, and Tacante explained. The Owl replied angrily, and Tacante translated.

"Maybe, he says," Tacante explained. "But we would kill all of you."

The wasicuns walked back to where the women and children remained. They discussed Hinhan Hota's words. The hairy-faced one returned alone.

"It's a fool leads married men to a gold camp," he said to Tacante. "We're goin' back."

Tacante shared the news with his father, and Hinhan Hota rose to his feet. The Owl then led the way to the horses. Once mounted, he waved his companions along. He left Hokala to watch, though.

"See that all of them go back," Hinhan Hota charged the Badger. "All. If any remain, come for us. Then there will be punishment."

Tacante witnessed the departure of the wagons himself. They struggled along the rock-strewn road, pursued by a small band of little ones. But there were no riders atop mules with them. Hokala soon appeared to confirm the news.

"They think we're fools not to notice," Hinhan Hota growled angrily when Badger explained how the party had separated. "We'll punish them now!"

He Hopa set about making medicine while the warriors dressed themselves for battle. Tacante smiled as he felt the three feathers woven into his long black hair. Hinhan Hota helped him paint face and chest. Together father and son tied up the tails of their best ponies, and brought along spares as well. Finally the warriors gathered to smoke the pipe.

"Wakan Tanka, look down upon us. Give us a good fight, for we ride to protect Uncle Buffalo and all his brother creatures. You make the earth rich and good, but these wasicuns would eat it all. Give us strong hearts."

"Hau!" the warriors shouted.

It didn't prove to be much of a battle. The Lakotas rode down on the wasicuns at a bend of the river and knocked them from their horses in the first charge. Quickly the startled white men were disarmed and led back to the wagons in triumph.

The wagons had gone but a short way before turning away from the river. Perhaps it was the hairy-faced wasicun's notion that such a trick would deceive the Lakotas. It only made them angry. Hinhan Hota led a charge which sent the little ones fleeing into the brush, screaming in terror. He counted coup on the hairy-faced one before dragging him from the seat of the wagon. The two women driving the second wagon abandoned it immediately. Then, in dismay, they watched the Lakotas tear off the canvas cover and take everything of value within. Hinhan Hota cut the oxen loose before setting the wagons ablaze.

The Owl then ordered the wasicuns herded between the blazing wagons. Tacante and Hokala had quite a challenge chasing down the younger children, for they scurried about the rocks like lizards. Finally they heeded their mothers' calls.

Hinhan Hota then addressed the captives with an angry voice, scolding them for their lies, warning that swift death would follow should they return to Powder River again.

"What's he goin' to do with us?" the hairy-faced leader asked Tacante. "Son, there are children no older'n seven years among us. Women, too."

"He knows this!" Tacante barked, motioning at his father.

Hinhan Hota then instructed the warriors to strip the captives. The men struggled a bit at first, but the sharp edge of a knife or the barrel of a gun persuaded them defiance was wasted. Tacante couldn't help laughing at the funny-looking wasicuns. Their arms and faces were tanned from the summer sun, but legs and chests and trunks were pale as moonlight. They were strangely hairy, with brownish curls on their chests as on their faces. Two even grew hair on their backs.

Hokala pulled some of this hair out by its roots, and a wasicun howled in pain. The Badger had thought it a medicine rite, decorating the body with hair like that.

When all the men were stripped, Hinhan Hota ordered the warriors to start on the women and children. Now there was great fighting. The women were determined to keep clothes, or some of them. One woman had so many layers it was thought a great mystery must lay beneath. Tacante wrestled with one of them long and hard before baring her back. She then bit his hand, causing him to yelp with pain.

The men were growing excited, too. No doubt the wasicuns imagined a terrifying fate lay ahead. In the end, one woman kept her undergarment, for it seemed painted to her hide and resisted every effort at removal. The other woman was allowed a dress, as she fought most bravely.

The little ones, once assured by Tacante they would not be taken from their mothers, reluctantly undressed. They resembled plucked prairie chickens, with skin so pale as to appear sickly. Tacante thought Wakan Tanka showed great wisdom painting wasicun bodies with hair, for they were too humorous a sight naked. Some covering was surely needed.

The final indignity befell the hairy-faced leader. Hinhan Hota ordered his hair cut so it no longer covered his ears. The wasicun remained stiff as a pine while knives clipped his hair.

Hinhan Hota shouted loudly, and Tacante again translated.

"He says now there is nothing to keep you from hearing!"

The Lakotas raised a great howl as they tossed the garments they didn't want onto the fiery wagon shells. Then Hinhan Hota pointed the way toward Platte River and left the naked wasicuns to find their way there.

It was a celebrated fight, for many mules and two horses were taken. The oxen were killed, and their meat cooked to make a feasting. All of the warriors had counted coups, and many stories were recounted around the fires of the hairy wasicuns. Itunkala sat beside Tacante and listened again and again to the tale of the woman with many dresses.

"Soon he will be ready to hunt," Hinhan Hota said when Tacante carried the Mouse inside the lodge and set him in his blankets. "He'll need a bow, a small one, for hunting rabbits. It should be made by a brother."

"I will do it, Ate," Tacante promised.

"You did well today, my son," the Owl praised. "Before, I worried you passed too much time with Hinkpila, speaking the wasicun words, learning of the strange ways. Now I see there is great worth to it. Soon we may all need such knowledge."

"These words are only needed to keep the wasicuns out," Tacante replied.

"Can a man stop a flood with only his two hands? I send these back to warn the others, but not all will see. I've watched the wagon trains beside Platte River. The wasicuns are many, and we are few."

"Wakan Tanka will give us brave hearts," Tacante declared.

"Ah, my brother had a brave heart," Hinhan Hota reminded Tacante. "He walked the sacred path all his days, but he is dead. I make prayers, but who can say what road Wakan Tanka sets before our feet?"

Tacante frowned as he lay upon his buffalo robes that night. Tasiyagnunpa spoke softly with the Owl, but Tacante couldn't hear the words. Wicatankala had gone to the women's lodge for the first time, and perhaps they spoke of this. Or maybe they wondered when Tacante would cut willow limbs and spread bunches of grass over them to make a wickiup as a young man did when he thought himself too old to remain in his father's lodge.

That time is coming, Tacante told himself. Even now Hokala dwelled in such a lodge. Cehupa Maza remained with his mother and surviving brothers, for there was no man to look to their needs. Tacante told himself there was Itunkala to look after, but in truth he found comfort trusting Hinhan Hota to choose the direction.

Often a man finds his direction chosen by others, though. So it was with Hinhan Hota's Sicangus. Waawanyanka, Watcher, arrived as the ripening moon of late summer began to wane.

"I bring word from Wapaha Luta," the young warrior explained gravely. "He makes war on the wasicuns soon."

"Han?" Hinhan Hota asked. Yes?

"Two times the sun has crossed the heavens since his daughter, Unkcekiha, was stolen from our camp. We rode to get her back, but there were many wasicun wagons. The Lance was wounded, and the warriors despaired. Come and help us make the good fight. We will rub out all of them!"

"All of them?" Tacante asked.

"There are forty, maybe more. Many are small and won't fight much," Watcher explained.

Hinhan Hota frowned. Tacante knew it wasn't in the Owl's heart to kill the helpless ones. There could be no refusing, though. Unkcekiha was He Hopa's granddaughter and a cousin to many of the young men. Hokala spoke of courting her if the bands reassembled to make their winter camp.

Word of Red Lance's trouble spread swiftly through the lodges of Gray Owl's camp, and the warriors made ready to ride. The Owl insisted some remain to guard the women and the horse herd. He chose Tacante, Hokala, and three others to go with him on the raid.

He Hopa would have gone if the Owl hadn't forbidden it.

"She's my blood," the medicine man argued.

"Ah, but your heart will be with us, just as your medicine charms will be," Hinhan Hota replied. "This is a young man's hunt, Leksi. See how I take only the swiftest riders?"

He Hopa grumbled some, but he accepted the decision. He did make prayers and assemble charms for the young warriors.

"Carry your shield high," the old man warned Hokala. "The wasicun rifles will seek your heart."

"Leave that pale horse behind," He Hopa told Tacante. "You must always wear dark paint and ride a black horse to battle, Tonska. Ah, four feathers are now in your hair."

He Hopa then did a strange thing. He drew a knife and cut Tacante's shoulder.

"Old man, leave my death to the wasicuns," Tacante barked.

"Ah, I have seen your blood in my dream," the medicine man explained. "Only one wound will you receive in this fight, and I have given it to you. No bullet will find you, Heart of the People. Ride with a brave heart, Tonska."

"I will do as you say, Leksi," Tacante said, referring to Four Horns as Uncle in the way Hinhan Hota and the elder Tacante before him had done.

He Hopa built a fire and made medicine. The warriors smoked the pipe and pledged their courage. Then they tied up the tails of their horses and set out after the wasicuns.

Two days Hinhan Hota kept them riding. They paused hardly long enough to eat, and certainly not long enough to sleep much. Often Tacante and the other young men dozed while their horses trotted onward. Each of the riders brought along a spare pony, and they shifted from one to the other so as to give the animals a rest. Gray Owl and Watcher had none.

The wasicun wagons had passed up the trail northward, but Wapaha Luta, wounded hip and all, kept up his pursuit. One wasicun had been captured while guarding the horse herd. Tacante saw what remained of him resting in a fire pit a half day's ride from the wagons.

"It was a boy," Tacante remarked as he stared at the blackened flesh.

"So, now there can be no talking," Hinhan Hota added. "Only fighting."

Often Tacante had imagined his first big fight. All boys do, he supposed. But he never envisioned charging wagons and battling wasicuns. The Crows, perhaps, or the Pawnees. He had little chance to consider it, though, for Hinhan Hota wasted no time in picking up the wasicun trail. Soon after midday they spotted the wagons. Red Lance arrived then, and a brief plan was made.

Warfare for the Lakotas was simple. Whenever a warrior felt the brave heart, he started a charge. If his medicine was strong, or he was respected, others would follow. The battle continued so long as there were brave hearts present, or until the enemy was driven off. Warriors preferred to count a coup, touch their bows to the enemy's shoulder, or slap him with the hand. White men who fired rifles were more often greeted with a deadly arrow fired from close range.

Most wagon trains formed squares or circles to defend themselves, thus blunting the charges and offering little chance for a horseman to close the range. But that day the wagons rumbled along their way in ignorance of the menace at hand, and there would be few opportunities to resist. Wapaha Luta, in spite of his broken hip and much loss of blood, led the first charge. He raced toward the middle of the wagon train, followed by Watcher and Black Dog. The three warriors swept past a startled outrider, who was promptly unhorsed by the Dog, and turned three wagons aside. A terrified young girl ran in front of a second wagon and was trampled by oxen. A boy no older than Itunkala stared up in surprise as a lance struck him down.

Wapaha Luta shouted a war cry, and the rest of the Lakotas charged. The wasicuns at the end of the wagon train had no chance to defend their wagons. Most abandoned everything and fled as fast as their feet would carry them. One man managed to load his rifle and fire at young Hokala, but while the blast gashed the tough hump hide of the shield, it left the warrior unharmed. Hinhan Hota struck the rifleman across the head, and he fell.

Unkcekiha, the Magpie, was found in the back of a wagon. Frightened and bewildered, but unhurt, she rejoiced at the sight of her people.

Hers was the only glad voice that day. The killing was great, with six white men slain and two women rubbed out, too. There was the trampled girl, too, and the boy killed by Wapaha Luta's lance. Already flames devoured several wagons, and the lumbering oxen were shot full of arrows. Then a line of wasicuns arrived from the front of the train, and they filled the air with their lead balls.

Sunkcincala Najin, Standing Colt, whose sister was Red Lance's wife, fell first, pierced by five bullets. Then Sunka Sapa howled as a ball penetrated the neck of his horse and lodged in the fleshy part of his right thigh.

Wapaha Luta, who did not know of his daughter's rescue, cried loudly as he hurled himself at the wasicuns. Bullets struck down the Lance's horse, then shattered his knee, broke his jaw, and severed three fingers from his left hand. Even so, the fiery-eyed warrior freed himself from his horse and struggled on. The whites drew back, but they managed to give the Lance two more wounds before breaking into flight. Only then did Wapaha Luta give up his life.

"Look there," Hokala called then, and Tacante spied a pair of wasicuns sneaking toward Hinhan Hota from behind. Tacante shouted a cry, notched an arrow, and rode swiftly toward the ambushers. Hokala was only a hair behind him, and the two young men ran down the wasicuns. Hokala jumped down and fired an arrow through the first wasicun's chest, killing him instantly.

Tacante took a bit longer dismounting. When his feet hit the ground, he found himself eyeing a thin-faced young man little older than himself. The wasicun fumbled with his pistol, and Tacante slapped it away. He then struck his enemy with the flat of the hand, and the young wasicun collapsed. His eyes were wild with fear, for he could see his companion lying dead a few feet away.

"Don't come again onto our land!" Tacante shouted as he took the pistol and stripped the wasicun of his cartridge belt. "You understand?"

The young enemy nodded. He attempted a smile, seeing that some miracle was allowing him to be spared.

"Go!" Tacante shouted, and the wasicun scrambled to his feet and fled for his life.

Now the fight was over. Warriors passed among the dead, counting coup or taking scalps. Only the hair of the trampled girl wasn't taken, for it seemed that Wakan Tanka had struck her down. In the distance the surviving wasicuns wailed as they watched their possessions burned and their companions marked with knives in the Lakota fashion.

Finally the dead were tied atop horses, and Hinhan Hota led the Lakotas from the bloody scene.

Chapter Eight

Moons rose and fell, and Tacante found himself a warrior of eighteen summers. Much had happened since Wapaha Luta's fight against the wasicun wagon train. The bluecoats had won their war in the faraway land, and once more the red man had become his enemy. Old Black Kettle's band of Southern Sahiyelas, known also as Cheyennes, had been cut down at Sand Creek, slain by bluecoats of the Colorado Territory's army. Worse, a peaceful Arapaho village had been razed in the Powder River country by a new bluecoat star chief. For days after word of the attacks reached Hinhan Hota's camp, Tacante's dreams filled with recollections of Blue Creek.

Great anger swelled inside the Lakotas. No longer did they ride out to scold the foolish wasicuns for trespassing onto land owned by the people. Bands of Sicangu and Oglala warriors painted their faces and tied up the tails of their horses. Sahiyela and Arapaho, too, joined the fight to keep the wasicun wagons from Powder River. Soon blood flowed freely.

Those were hard days for all, but more so for Tacante. He felt tall and proud, a man in all important ways, but he looked upon a world torn by change. Each summer the buffalo herds dwindled. The roads were full of wasicuns. The singing wires that followed Platte River westward foretold the death of the free life.

Once a young man of eighteen summers would only have concerned himself with hunting and perhaps searching for a wife. Tacante had fifteen horses, and there were girls among the Sicangus and Oglalas both who had ears for his flute and eyes for his shy grin.

"Toskala is a pretty one," Itunkala, his brother, said. "I have heard her say she admires your skill with the bow. Her father would not want so many ponies, for he has many daughters to feed."

Tacante gazed at his small brother's laughing face and pretended anger.

"It's for me to choose!" he barked. "It's not good for a warrior, risking death each day, to take a young wife, to bring little ones into a dark time."

"I, your brother, would look to them while you're gone," Itunkala offered, grinning mightily. Tacante gave his brother's scalp a yank in answer.

But as the prairie grasses greened, Tacante was more and more preoccupied with the courtship practices. Sometimes he would sit with Hokala on the ridge above the stream and wait for the maidens to pass on their way to fetch water. Sometimes Hokala, who was far bolder, might notch a bird arrow on his bowstring and shoot a hole in a water skin or perhaps drop willow leaves into a girl's hair. The maidens would cry out and pursue their tormentors. Sometimes Hokala was rewarded with a stone in the back or a thrashing with cottonwood limbs. Tacante preferred to tease the girls, though once he dug a bear pit to trap Pehan, the Crane Girl.

Mostly these games were for acquainting a young warrior with the maidens from whom he might choose a wife. After all, a girl changed greatly from the time she first entered the women's lodge. Once Tacante had thought nothing of splashing naked in the river with the girls of the tribe close by. Now the old women, who were forever watchful, would see such an act punished. Great care had to be taken with the hawk-eyed old crows about!

Formal courtship was another matter. In the evening, a young man might appear outside a maiden's lodge with a blanket. If her father agreed, a maiden might sit beside her caller while he pulled the blanket over them. Perhaps the two would tease each other or carry on talk of the future. If the blanket enclosed them too long, a mother or aunt would pull the two apart and scold them for their misdeed.

Tacante appeared with his blanket beside the lodge of Toskala, the Downy Woodpecker, but others were there, too, and her father hardly gave a glance to young Buffalo Heart. Once he did sit with Hetkala, the Squirrel, but she devoted their time to giggling and tracing her fingers along the old scar on Tacante's elbow.

"Ah, how is it girls can make a man so crazy!" Tacante cried to his father.

"There are mysteries never revealed," Hinhan Hota replied. "And this is a great one, indeed. Be patient, my son. There is always the hunt."

That was surely true. But no sooner did Hinhan Hota's reunited band set out upon the buffalo range than a youthful rider appeared.

"Hinkpila!" Tacante shouted as Louis Le Doux raised his hand in greeting. "Hau, kola!"

"Hau, kola," Louis answered. "Welcome, my brother. Ate," he added, turning to the Owl. "I bring word of a gathering of the people."

"What gathering is this?" Hinhan Hota asked, halting the hunters.

"Wasicun chiefs come to talk of peace," Louis explained. "Too many have died on Powder River. All the Lakotas are coming in. Already the Oglalas and Minikowojus, the Hunkpapas and Sihasapas are there. Cheyennes and Arapahos, even some Crows, are camping together. Never have so many lodges blackened the plain!"

"They talk of peace?" Hinhan Hota asked, shaking his head in confusion. "Already they send their wagons into our country. The star chief has built a fort beside Powder River. We know this wasicun way. He talks of peace while he sharpens the long knife to kill our children."

"Red Cloud comes," Louis told them. "He has sworn to fight the road. Maybe the wasicuns don't understand."

"A man with no ears to hear will never understand," Hinhan Hota replied. "But we will come and listen. And while we sit in council, the wasicuns will steal more of our country."

Other bands said much the same, but even so, they came to Fort Laramie in great numbers that summer the wasicuns called 1866. Tacante shared his father's feelings, but the peace speakers distributed many presents. And it was good to pass days again in the company of Hinkpila, his kola.

The brother-friends rode the far hills in search of game for the kettles, and they shared many stories. Louis told of traveling east to the big wasicun village called St. Louis. Much of this journey was made riding inside the iron horse. Ah, this horse was faster than the swiftest Lakota pony, and it could ride for days with scarcely a rest. It ate cottonwood logs and breathed smoke.

Tacante laughed at such an old woman's tale. Monsters that spit smoke and fire were for scaring little ones. Tacante had seen the blue-coat thunder guns!

When not hunting or admiring maidens, the two young men joined in the many contests. Often in the evenings Tacante would join his Oglala friends as they displayed their horsemanship. Warriors would ride beneath the bellies of their horses or on one side. Some would stand on the back or rump of an animal, or even set one foot on each of two galloping stallions. Others jumped on and off their mounts, displaying amazing acrobatic talents. The peace speakers shouted their astonishment and proclaimed that surely the Indian was the most masterful of horsemen.

The tribes warmed under such praise, and with their women satisfied with shiny-looking glasses and strings of trade beads, there was much good feeling for the wasicuns. The post traders exchanged new rifles for buffalo hides, and even the pitiful Arapahos, whose camps had been so recently destroyed, had fresh lead and powder for the summer hunting.

"See how the wasicuns pay for their misdeeds?" some asked.

But when the terms of the new treaty were revealed, those same voices spoke with bad hearts. The wasicuns, who had cut their road across the people's land, had killed so many Sahiyelas and Arapahos, now demanded a permanent road with forts full of soldiers in the heart of the Big Horn country.

"You ask us to touch the pen to this paper?" Red Cloud asked. "You promise us presents and say these other lands will be ours forever. Many of us touched the pen before to a paper saying you would never come to Powder River, that you would make no roads and build no forts there. These promises you have broken. Your word is worthless. I will never give up these lands. Already the buffalo is gone from Platte River. You would take our last good hunting grounds. Some will fight you. I will lead them!"

Red Cloud wasn't the only Lakota to speak. The warriors mounted their horses and rode around the fort, raising a great cloud of dust and frightening the peace speakers. Then, even as the tribes waited for blankets promised as presents, a large column of bluecoats appeared.

"They've come to build the road and garrison the new forts," Louis told Tacante.

"Then they've come to die," Tacante said, his heart sour with bitterness. "Never before have so many seen and heard the bad words of the wasicun. Here, while some speak of peace, others come to steal what they cannot buy!"

Red Cloud and the other chiefs said much the same thing to the wasicun peace speakers. Only a few loaf-around-the-fort Lakotas agreed to touch the pen. The Crows signed, but they had no reason to object to the treaty; it wasn't their land.

Soon the great encampment at Fort Laramie broke up. Bands went north or west, onto the plain or into the mountains. Some made a summer camp in some place of safety, then sent the warriors to Powder River. Red Cloud's Oglalas headed for the wasicun fort built near where Powder River's forks flowed into the main stream. Hinhan Hota followed the Cloud. Tacante rode at his side.

"I want to be with my people," Tacante told Louis.

"There is no use fighting so many," Louis argued. "I hoped we would hunt the buffalo this summer. Kolas should not be so far parted."

"No," Tacante agreed, gripping his brother-friend's hands. "We should visit the maidens on their water walk by the river, wrapping ourselves in blankets with the pretty ones."

"Yes. Maybe it will be a short war, and there can be peace again soon."

"Maybe," Tacante said, not believing it for a moment. They both knew that soon the Heart of the People must be shooting arrows at bluecoat soldiers. And Hinkpila, whose high cheeks and brownish flesh marked him as his Lakota grandmother's kin, would sell goods to the new wave of wasicuns traveling Platte River, many of them headed up the stolen road toward the Yellowstone country.

Soon the wasicun soldiers moved west. There were too many of them to fight at one time, so scouts kept watch, waiting for a chance to strike. Among the young men sent to look were Hokala and Tacante. They rode with a clever Oglala called Heca, the Buzzard. Heca possessed a yellow powder that he smeared on his bare chest before approaching the wasicun camps. The powder was powerful medicine, for it blinded the wasicuns from seeing Buzzard. He could come and go but never be seen. Hau, that was strong medicine, Tacante thought.

Soon other scouts appeared to watch the wasicuns, and Tacante joined his father and a band of warriors sent to get meat for the starving moons of winter. Hunting was good, and by midsummer the wasna pouches were full. The Owl then joined his Oglala friends on Powder River. Tacante and Hokala rode to spy on the wasicun fort, for all the bluecoats had gathered there. A trader had left his horses to graze on a nearby hill, and the young Lakotas gazed upon the ponies with big eyes. In an instant they were riding up that hill, and before the foolish trader could raise an alarm, his ponies were running off to join the Lakota herds.

A small party of bluecoats set out on Tacante's trail, but they soon halted. The Lakotas watched them from atop a ridge and shouted insults. An Oglala bared his backside in disdain, for here were wasicuns wearing war shirts who could not fight an old woman!

The bluecoats paused but a short while at this fort. The half-starved soldiers already there went back down the road. Others replaced them. Then the rest of them moved north, into the Big Horns.

For a time the Lakotas satisfied themselves with stealing a horse or raiding the wasicun gold seekers. Sometimes a few wagons crept up the road alone. They made fine fires. If the men escaped, it was not so bad, for they found the soldiers and told terrible tales to spread fear.

On a place called Piney Creek, the wasicuns built a second fort. These forts were peculiar, for always before the wasicuns had put up rows of buildings in their crazy squares. Unlike the sacred circle of lodges that made up a Lakota camp, there were always big lodges and small ones, their size speaking of the importance the wasicuns placed upon the owners. The forts on the stolen road were different, for around the lodges the bluecoats built high walls of pointed sticks. It was hard to come and go, and the Lakotas laughed.

"See how the wasicuns build their own cages!" Hokala exclaimed.

Yes, Tacante thought. For soon these forts were jails. The Lakotas made it hard for even the small wood-cutting parties to leave. And not long after the wall was finished, the Oglalas made a raid on the pony herd, stealing a hundred horses and many mules.

"Now they will stay here!" Hinhan Hota declared angrily. "Our helpless ones will be safe in their camps. When the snows come, these wasicuns will freeze here. There is not enough meat to fill their bellies, and we won't let them hunt. Hau! They will suffer like my brother."

Such was the talk among the Lakotas. Even Tacante, who often watched the fort from the high ridge nearby, was eaten up with anger. Why had the wasicuns come into the Big Horn country, driving out the elk and the deer with their great noisy wagons? Why had they forgotten their promises? If all of them died, even the smallest child, no Lakota heart would sadden. For their hearts had turned bad toward the wasicuns.

Chapter Nine

Tacante and the other young Sicangus occupied themselves watching the wasicun fort. Many bluecoats slept inside the high walls, and Hinhan Hota warned of the folly in attacking such a strong place. Better to let the wasicuns come out and fight in open country.

Mahpiya Luta, Red Cloud, was of the same mind. The Oglala chief was now looked upon as war leader, for he spoke with wisdom and determination. It was nothing to let the wasicuns sleep in their wooden cage. Let them grow cold and hungry with the approaching snows. But whenever the bluecoats emerged to cut wood or hunt game, the Lakota watchers sent word. Soon a war party was snapping at the soldiers' heels.

Tacante, Hokala, Cehupa Maza, and their old friends Sunka Sapa and Waawanyanka were among those who joined in the raids on the woodcutters. Tacante felt proud that five young men from his father's camp should strike at the hated wasicuns. A large group of Oglalas came as well, led by a light-skinned young warrior known as Sunkawakan Witkotkoke, the Confused or Crazed Horse. The Oglalas already sang of his bravery, for he had fought well against the Crows and the Snakes.

He was a strange one, Tacante observed. Unlike his companions, the Horse wore few decorations into battle. He stripped himself naked save for a modest breechclout, and other than wearing a red-tailed hawk in his hair and painting numerous hailstones on his chest, he was little different from the untried boys who came along to look after the spare ponies.

Once in a fight, though, Sunkawakan Witkotkoke was a man to notice. Often he led the charge, and he was always the last to leave the enemy. His medicine bent the paths of bullets so that he could ride unharmed, and those who followed such strong medicine enjoyed success.

All this Tacante learned from the young Oglalas who followed the strange one toward the ridge where bluecoats were felling cottonwoods. Once the Lakotas grew near, the Horse called for silence.

"Who will follow me to decoy the soldiers?" Sunkawakan Witkotkoke asked. "Hau! It's a good day to die!"

The others shouted eagerly, and the Horse chose three Oglalas for the decoys. While the rest of the raiders hid themselves in a ravine and waited, the decoys cautiously approached the woodcutters and called out a challenge.

These wasicuns knew little about fighting, for they quickly abandoned their work and began firing their rifles. The Horse was clever. He rode just beyond the rifles' range, shouting and taunting the soldiers. When five of them at last mounted horses and set off in pursuit, Tacante felt his blood rise.

The big, grain-fed American horses were no match for plains ponies, and Crazy Horse often had to slow his pace so that the pursuing wasicuns would not lose heart and turn back. Then when the decoys passed the ravine, their companions emerged, firing arrows or bullets at the astonished wasicuns. One bluecoat fell immediately, and Hokala hurried to count coup on him. Another wasicun then turned and raced toward the unsuspecting Badger.

"Hau!" Tacante screamed, charging to intercept the wasicun. The bluecoat heard Tacante's galloping horse and managed to fire a shot. The bullet sliced a path through Buffalo Heart's ankle, but the young man swallowed his pain and raised his captured pistol. He fired at the wasicun, and the bluecoat's head snapped back. For a moment powder smoke obscured the scene. When Tacante broke through the sulfuric haze, he saw the soldier lying on the ground, his face bloody and his eyes frozen in death.

"Hau!" Tacante's companions shouted as he jumped to the ground and counted coup on the corpse.

"Take his scalp," Hokala advised, holding up the scalp lock of the first dead soldier.

"Hau, mark him in the Lakota way!" Sunka Sapa added.

Tacante gazed down at the lifeless soldier. He wasn't old and hairy-faced like the ones at Fort Laramie. His glazed eyes were blue like summer sky, and his hair was almost yellow. Two medicine stripes marked his shirt. Ah, he was a minor chief, and yet so young! Hau, it was a brave heart who could kill such a wasicun.

Tacante knew what he now must do, but the cutting didn't come easily to him. The anger in his heart born at Blue Creek wasn't strong now. He found himself wondering about the dead wasicun. Was there a wife and children? Perhaps he had a young brother to show the manhood ways.

"More are coming!" Waawanyanka cried. Watcher was always the keen-eyed one, and he'd spotted a column of bluecoats riding hard from the fort. Tacante swallowed hard, drove his knife below the hairline, and cut the small square of scalp from the bluecoat's head. He then held the yellow hair up for his admiring companions to view. Sunka Sapa pounced upon the corpse and opened a gash on the soldier's thigh. It was the way Lakotas marked their enemies. When such men's shades limped on the other side, all would know it was a brave heart Lakota who made it so.

"Tacante, Hokala," Sunkawakan Witkotkoke called. "Follow me!"

The young men scrambled atop their ponies and rode after the Horse. The three of them became decoys now, but the soldiers had chased enough. Two of them were dead, and another was struck in the hip by an arrow. The bluecoats recovered their dead and turned back toward the woodcutters.

Many would have been satisfied with the victory, but Crazy Horse turned his attention again to the woodcutters. He left his horse with the boys and led the young men up the hill where the soldiers were chopping cottonwoods. Soon a cutter howled out in pain as an arrow bit into his neck. Another cutter was pierced through the heart and fell dead. It was as if the hillside had come alive with silent death. Lakotas could stand, fire an arrow, and hide again before the dull-eyed wasicuns took notice.

Silent death struck again and again until the woodcutters threw down their axes and fled.

Hokala and Cehupa Maza hurled insults at the escaping cowards. Sunkawakan Witkotkoke knelt beside Tacante's foot and examined the wound, which was now bleeding freely.

"Little brother, there are few brave hearts. It's not good to count coup and bleed to death the same instant!"

It was Crazy Horse's way to make light of a wound, to scold in a friendly manner. The Horse cut a slice of fresh elk meat he carried in his food bag and placed it over the gash. Then he bound the wound with rawhide strips.

"See it is tended," Sunkawakan Witkotkoke advised. "Soon we'll teach the wasicuns another trick."

"Hau!" Tacante responded. He mounted his horse and headed toward the distant lodge of his father. Waawanyanka and Sunka Sapa returned to their watching hill. Hokala and Cehupa Maza accompanied their wounded friend homeward.

"We've become great warriors today," Hokala sang, waving his scalp.

Tacante tried to smile in agreement, but it wasn't possible. He felt only hollowness, for killing weighed heavily on some. Tacante's friends thought him weak from pain, but the ankle barely throbbed now. It was the haunting eyes of the yellow-haired wasicun that plagued him. And the knowledge that other bluecoats must die before the Lakotas regained their lands.

Their return to the camp brought cries of thanksgiving and shouts of triumph. Hokala rushed off to present his scalp to his eldest sister, leaving Cehupa Maza to assist Tacante to his father's lodge. Hinhan Hota received his son with a stern but approving gaze. Little Itunkala examined the clump of yellow hair and set off to boast to the other boys of his brother's triumph.

"This is for my sister, Wicatankala," Tacante said when the Gull appeared. She took the scalp reverently, then gazed at Tacante's bound ankle.

"My brother's done a great thing," she declared, holding the scalp high so all the assembled Sicangus could see it. "Now is the time for rest and food. Surely He Hopa's medicine will bring a fast healing."

He Hopa, hearing his name, hobbled through the crowd. Seeing Tacante and the bloodstained wrapping, he waved his hands to disperse the crowd, then motioned for Cehupa Maza and Hinhan Hota to bring the wounded young man along. He Hopa limped back to his lodge and ducked inside. Tacante, resting now in the firm hands of father and friend, was brought along inside.

He Hopa was already chanting and throwing bits of powder upon a small flame. The fire changed from red to blue to white as it devoured the mystic fuel. He Hopa chanted, then sourly turned his attention to the foot.

"Ah, it's often spoken that pain is a great teacher," the old man muttered as he cut the rawhide straps and exposed the wound. "A man lives longer who doesn't rush toward wasicun bullets."

"Yes," Hinhan Hota agreed as he sternly held his son down while He Hopa drew a knife and cut along the edge of a blackish section of flesh. The skin bled as he scraped particles of lead and powder from the swollen tissues. Then he cut the misshapen ball from where it rested against the tip of the lower leg bone.

"Tell the girl to bring water," He Hopa bellowed, and Cehupa Maza rushed out to do it. Moments later a young woman appeared with a water skin, and He Hopa bathed the wound.

"It smells good, and the blood is very red," He Hopa announced, peppering yellow powder over the wound. "Now I will bind it."

Tacante winced as He Hopa applied a section of deerhide over the ankle and then laced it tight with sinew. The ankle rebelled against the binding, and pain shot up Tacante's leg.

"Yes, pain is a good teacher," He Hopa said, laughing at his young companion's discomfort. "Girl, bring food," he barked, and the young woman rushed out to the cook fire.

Tacante gazed through the oval entrance to the tipi and watched as she bent over a kettle. She was rather skinny, and very shy. Even so, her eyes seemed to sparkle a bit when she noticed him watching.

"My Oglala granddaughter," He Hopa explained, grinning. "She's called Hehaka."

Deer woman? Tacante took another long look. Her bare legs were lean and powerful, and she seemed at ease stirring the kettle.

"Her father's lodge is full of young women," He Hopa said, turning

Tacante's head away. "Too many for the old women to watch. He sends me this one to learn the healing herbs, not to waste her time on the water path or wrapped in your blanket."

"She's too skinny," Tacante said, laughing. "And I'm too young."

"Ah, I read your thoughts, Heart of the People," He Hopa answered. "Keep your eyes to the warrior path. I'll look after Hehaka."

"Han, Leksi," Tacante said, knowing the old man knew what was best.

Still, as the healing days continued, and the ankle grew whole again, Tacante had much time for thought. Hehaka avoided his eyes whenever her grandfather was near, but when with the other maidens, she often flashed a shy smile in Tacante's direction.

"Take care, my son," Hinhan Hota warned. "Her father is Wanbli Cannunpa."

"Ah," Tacante said, digesting the news. Eagle Pipe was a feared warrior and a well-known chief among the Oglalas. He would tolerate no foolishness from his daughters, or from others, either. Still, the daughter of the Pipe would bring brave heart sons into the world. Tacante admired Hehaka all the more.

It was not a time for courting young women or dreaming of the future, though. The wasicuns continued to send wood gatherers out into the distant hills, or parties to shoot fresh meat, and Mahpiya Luta was determined to make them bleed. Once Tacante was able to walk without opening his wound, Hokala urged him to return to the ridge.

"Han!" Tacante said eagerly. Yes, it was time to be a watcher again. A warrior, after all, had obligations.

Mostly the woodcutters traveled in large bands now, and their guards kept together. Oh, sometimes a wasicun strayed. Perhaps he went off to relieve himself behind a cottonwood or to fetch water from a spring. Often the wasicuns did so rapidly and returned long before a watcher could sneak among the trees and take his life. If the bluecoats were lazy or wandered a little, they died.

Still, the best way to win a victory was to decoy a large band of the soldiers into a trap. Sunkawakan Witkotkoke invited Tacante and Hokala to join the decoys again and again. There were many hot bloods among the soldiers, and often their voices called upon the bluecoat chiefs to charge. Among the wasicuns there was a wary-eyed one, though, and even the best traps couldn't tempt him to chase.

"White cowards!" Tacante sometimes shouted at the reluctant cavalrymen. "We are only three, and you are many. Come and fight us!"

The soldiers cried in anger, but their chief only laughed. He had the far-seeing medicine, it was said, and he wouldn't follow the decoys.

As the air grew chill, and the leaves yellowed and began falling from the cottonwoods, a great impatience rose among the Lakotas. The Big Horn country was not a favored winter camp. Many of the Sicangus and Minikowojus had left the shadow of the wasicun fort to find better water. Other bands sent their women and little ones to shelter, for the heavy snows would come soon. Warriors young and old stayed, for Mahpiya Luta spoke strong words, and many of the young men had counted coup.

Sunkawakan Witkotkoke was restless. He spoke little to his companions, but all who saw the strange Oglala knew many thoughts crossed his mind. Finally he gathered a band of the young men and rode north along the white man's road.

"See," the Horse said, pointing to fresh tracks in the muddy path. "Many wagons and horses come and go here. Our watchers on the road don't have the all-seeing eyes."

"We will watch for the wasicun wagons," Hokala volunteered.

"Hau, we'll all watch," Sunkawakan Witkotkoke declared. "And we'll make these wasicuns turn away from our country."

"Or die," a Sahiyela cried, raising his bow high. The Sahiyelas were still mourning the deaths at Sand Creek, and their young men were eager to charge the bluecoats. They trusted the Horse to make good plans, though, and they agreed to be patient.

Sunkawakan Witkotkoke spaced his watchers carefully, and it wasn't long before Sunka Sapa spotted wagons. The Horse gathered his warriors and rode out to have a look. The Lakotas and their Sahiyela companions were disappointed to see a band of twenty soldiers riding with the five wagons.

"Brave up!" Sunkawakan Witkotkoke called. "Who rides with me to decoy the bluecoats?"

Tacante raised his bow, as did many others. Crazy Horse chose two Sahiyelas, Tacante, and an Oglala called Maka. While the others gathered along the road ahead, the five decoys charged the soldiers.

"Hau! It's a good day to die," Sunkawakan Witkotkoke cried, as he always did. The decoys swept over a hill and were among the soldiers in an instant. The Horse fired his rifle into the face of a three-striped wasicun, then shot another bluecoat with a pistol. A wasicun rifle dropped Maka, the Skunk, but most of the soldiers were too surprised to shoot. Tacante guided his buckskin horse by pressing his knees while he notched one arrow after another and fired into the confused escort. The soldiers scattered a moment, then collected their wits and set out in pursuit of the Lakotas.

"Upelo!" Tacante yelled to the waiting ambushers. "They're coming!"

Sunkawakan Witkotkoke couldn't have planned it better. As the cavalrymen hurried toward the waiting ambush, the Horse peeled off into the pines with his companions and raced back toward the wagons. The soldiers thundered on down the road. Even as the former decoys approached the defenseless wagons, wild Lakota war shouts mixed with the cries of dying wasicun soldiers to create an unearthly sound.

The wagon people looked on anxiously as the Lakotas neared. Tacante searched the faces of the drivers, noted grimly the bundled women and children staring out from beneath the canvas covers, and grew sad. These wasicuns weren't soldiers. They'd been foolish to come, but perhaps they would turn away.

Sunkawakan Witkotkoke pulled up his horse, and Tacante halted as well. The two Lakotas seemed of one mind. These wasicuns should turn away. The Sahiyelas only wanted blood. They raised their bows and charged. One wagon driver leaped from his seat and fled. The others fought to form a square with their wagons, but the road was narrow there, and time was short. The first Sahiyela flung himself at the second wagon and drove a knife into the heart of its driver. The second cut the horses loose from the back wagon so that the trail was blocked in both directions.

"Hau, little brother!" the Horse shouted as he slid his rifle into a deerskin sheath and drew out a buffalo-killing lance. "It's a good day to die."

For them, Tacante thought as he kicked his horse into a gallop. But this is no brave heart fight. It's only killing.

As Tacante suspected, there was little fighting to it. The drivers were all dead or dying by the time the Heart reached the wagons. Some of the women fought to protect their young ones, and a few of the older boys and girls tried to load and fire old rifles. They were accustomed to shooting deer or birds, though, not firing on a charging Sahiyela or Lakota warrior.

Tacante contented himself at first with running down the lead driver. Here, after all, was a coward that earned death. An arrow through the back felled the fugitive. Tacante refused to touch the scalp of such a weak-hearted man.

When he returned to the wagons, the Horse motioned toward a pair of fleeing figures on the far side of the road. One stumbled and fell, but the other ran on. Tacante judged the wasicun to be a boy of fourteen summers. The Heart would have let him escape had not the wasicun produced a pistol and fired.

"Ayyy!" Tacante shouted as he whipped his horse onward. The boy turned and ran, but there was no escaping. Tacante swung his bow, tripping the young man so that he fell hard against the rocky ground. The young Sicangu jumped down, drew a knife, and pounced on his victim.

"God, no," the young man pleaded as Tacante grabbed a handful of light brown hair. "Mama? Papa?"

Tacante hesitated. His heart seemed to empty as he beheld a weeping face. The boy wore spectacles. Eyeglasses!

"Istamaza?" Tacante muttered, recalling the Lakota name given to Hinkpila's younger brother.

The young wasicun tried to stop his tears. He managed a faint grin.

"Plllease, lllet me . . . go," he stammered. "I, uh, nnnever, uh, oh, God!"

The boy looked behind him, and Tacante glanced in time to see one of the Sahiyelas tear a yellow dress from the shoulders of a young girl, the same one who had followed the boy down the road.

"Katie!" the boy cried as he groped under his knee for something. The pistol! The gun's barrel suddenly exploded, sending a projectile slicing past Tacante's head. The boy tried to fire again, but Tacante turned the barrel, and the bullet struck instead the young wasicun low in the belly. The boy grunted as he dropped the gun and gazed at the wide hole in his abdomen.

"God, I'm kilt," he said, falling back.

Tacante angrily gripped the wasicun's forelock and cut it away. He barely heard the resulting howl.

"Hau, Tacante!" Hokala shouted as he rode by holding the scalp of a wasicun soldier. The Badger wore a blue soldier shirt loosely about his otherwise bare shoulders.

A band of Sahiyelas now hurried over the scene, gazing at the corpses.

"Ah, he'll soon die," one said as he looked upon the spectacled boy.

"Not so quickly as he'll wish," another added as he drew a knife. The other Sahiyela began stripping the bleeding wasicun's clothes. Then two knives set to work, severing fingers, opening new wounds on the trunk, slicing an ear. . . .

Tacante could stand to watch no longer. He got to his feet and hurried toward his horse. Back where the wagons stood, Cehupa Maza and Sunka Sapa kindled a fire that would soon swallow the vehicles. Waawanyanka, as was his habit, sat atop his horse and watched the distant horizon for sign of the enemy.

Tacante joined him.

"You've counted coup," the Watcher observed.

Tacante stared at the bloody thing in his hand, then glanced back to where the Sahiyelas continued to cut other pieces off its owner. The wasicuns at Sand Creek had performed terrible, sickening acts upon the Sahiyelas, Tacante had learned. Women were cut open, and men's parts were cut off to be displayed as trophies. This was not war the way the old men sang of it. Where was respect for a brave heart enemy?

"He was no older than my sister," Tacante muttered. "He fought as he could, but he was young. Now the Sahiyelas cut him apart."

"They have bad hearts from Sand Creek," Watcher said, and Tacante nodded. "We fought the bluecoats hard, but half got away. More may come soon from the fort."

"Then we must go," Tacante said, gazing at the madness all around him. "We're few now to fight many."

"So talks the Horse, but the Sahiyelas will not leave, and his medicine won't let him go if they stay."

Yes, it was a leader's way to see his warriors safely away. But to risk death for the sake of such doings was crazy! It was why so many followed Sunkawakan Witkotkoke, though, Tacante decided. For none among them would ever be left behind.

Chapter Ten

There was little time to celebrate the victory over the wagon train people and the soldiers. Even as Tacante joined in the scalp dance, dark clouds choked the heavens, and the first icy winds of winter descended upon the plains.

Ah, it's right for winter to come, Tacante told himself. For surely a season of death had come to the Big Horn country. Hardly a day passed now when the woodcutters weren't attacked or wasicuns were killed on the road. There would be no more parleys, no warnings given, either, for three Oglala boys fishing Powder River had been shot by wagon people. Now any wasicun daring to cross Lakota land was killed at the first chance.

He Hopa called it the bad heart winter and painted it so on his winter count.

"Ah, that's work for the old ones," Tacante told the medicine man when he saw He Hopa scratching pigment on the smooth side of a buffalo hide. "You have many winters yet to remember."

"Not many," the old man argued. "The cold eats at my marrow, and the power escapes my dreams. Already others make the cures. Soon I, too, will be dust."

It saddened Tacante to think of a world without He Hopa, the Four

Horns. The Heart knew no grandfather, for his was a warrior line, and the men too often fell in the hard fights against the Crows or to wasicun treachery.

Tacante watched He Hopa's step slow as the wind whined and the snows fell. And each time the trilling of the women announced a death in the camp, the Heart of the People prayed it to be someone else.

"What will come of us if you go away?" Tacante asked one afternoon as the sun briefly chased off the clouds and warmed the earth.

"I no longer see what will come," He Hopa answered. "It's for the young men with power, those like you, Heart of the People, to search their dreams. Mine are clouded by creeping death."

Tacante somberly accepted that word. When night fell, he ate nothing but a few strips of wasna, dried buffalo meat, wrapped himself in his thickest elk robe, and set out alone on the snow-covered ground. When his legs began to grow numb, he stopped and stared overhead. The sky was clear for a time, and stars gazed down upon the earth.

"Hear me, Sky Father," Tacante pleaded as he discarded his robe. He then slipped his shirt over his shoulders so that flakes of drifting snow danced across his bare chest. "Send me a vision that I may look to the welfare of the people." The cold ate at him, numbing his fingers and then his arms. It was all he could manage to stand. Tacante knew cold could induce fever, though, and a fever often brought on a dreaming. If death came first, then still his plea would have had an answer.

Again and again he called out to the dim lights above. Sky Father, who had joined with Mother Earth in the beginning to make the first creatures, was generous. Often he took men to the other side, among those who had passed over, so that what was to come could be seen. But as Tacante's sight blurred and frost whitened his face, no hand reached out to draw him to the other side.

Finally there was an immense nothingness. Tacante felt himself floating, and he wondered if this was death. A voice whispered to him in an unknown tongue. And then the dream came.

There was a long, flat hill beside the wasicun road, but where usually the pines and cottonwoods grew, a forest of feathers now bloomed. These feathers grew arms, and each arm held a killing lance.

"These I give to you," a voice called out, and a massive hand opened up. One by one a hundred naked wasicuns fell like snowflakes onto the hill. They lay there, side by side. Then a delicate white blanket fell over them, and their eyes were closed as in death.

When Tacante awoke, the vision still flooded his mind. He tried to rise, but a firm hand pressed him flat against a stack of buffalo robes.

"No!" a young feminine face ordered. "You must rest."

He blinked away confusion and fatigue. As his eyes focused, he recognized Hehaka, the Deer Woman.

"I . . . I . . ." Tacante began.

"You were lost in the snows," He Hopa said, joining them. "Fool of a boy, winter can swallow the young as well as the old."

"I sought a vision," Tacante explained.

"Ah, bringing death close is a way," the old man said, laughing to himself. "Better to call Wakan Tanka to give you power."

"The dreaming came," Tacante said then, and He Hopa grew solemn.

"Leave us," the medicine man bellowed, and Hehaka scurried to the far side of the snowbound lodge. "What did you see?" he asked Tacante.

"Much, Leksi," Tacante explained. The young warrior then recounted the dream exactly as it had come. He Hopa scowled for a moment, then nodded.

"It tells much," the medicine man said. "There comes a fight. The feathers are warriors lying in ambush. The wasicuns are dead soldiers slain on this hill. Wakan Tanka sends the people a victory over our enemies. A hundred slain! Never have the wasicuns suffered so!"

"Then I must return to the fort," Tacante said, feeling still the effects of his exposure. "It will take many warriors to fight and kill so many bluecoats."

"You must go, as must the other young men," He Hopa agreed. "But first you will rest and make your body whole once more."

"No, He Hopa. I must hurry."

"Wakan Tanka gives the people a victory, Heart of the People. It is not won by you and your brothers alone. Trust in your dreaming, Nephew. All will be as the dream foretold."

So it was that Tacante and the other young men waited a week before riding back across Powder River and up the stolen road into the Big Horns. Nights were bitter cold, and grass was scarce. The horses were hungry most of the time. In the end, though, Tacante's small band joined a growing mass that had gathered to fight the wasicuns.

"I've had a dream," Tacante explained to Sunkawakan Witkotkoke when the strange one greeted him.

"As have others," the Horse said, pointing to the hundreds of warriors. "You will ride with the decoys?"

"Always," Tacante volunteered.

The plan was an old one. Lead the soldiers to a place from which there was no escaping, and fall upon them without mercy. Always before the bluecoat chiefs had ignored the bait. Decoys taunted and insulted, but the soldiers refused to give chase.

A different wasicun chief commanded the bluecoats this time, though. Afterward it was learned this wasicun, who had fought in the war against the graycoats as an eagle chief, boasted he and eighty soldiers could ride down all the Lakotas if given the chance. Now the chance came, but the spirits never favor the boastful.

Tacante followed Sunkawakan Witkotkoke that eventful day. Hokala was at one side, and Cehupa Maza rode at the other. Loud was the howling as the Lakotas taunted the soldiers. Finally the bluecoat chief ordered his horns to blow. The soldiers formed a line and galloped off after the decoys.

The trap was well laid, on the long hill Tacante had seen in his dream. It was a long way, and the decoys risked much as they slowed to let the bluecoats come close. One band of soldiers rode poor mules, and few of their horses were as good as Tacante's. Shots often whizzed through the air. One hit Cehupa Maza in the leg, but he who was called Iron Jaw had an iron will, too. The bleeding Sicangu kept pace in spite of his pain.

Finally the decoys passed the watching ridge and headed toward the long hill. They climbed the slope with fresh spirit, for here waited their brothers. "Upelo! Upelo!" the decoys shouted again and again. They come!

Along came the great column of bluecoats. Their horses struggled to climb the hill. Onward and onward they came. Then, atop the hill, the decoys stopped. Again came the taunts, but this time the words were spoken as to a foolish child.

"You who would spoil the world with your stolen roads and wood-walled forts, sing a death song. For here the Lakotas will kill you!"

The decoys charged down the slope, leaving the foolish wasicuns encircled by a great host of Lakotas.

At first the bluecoats stumbled about in confusion. One part rode onward toward the far end of the hill. They were soon halted by a wave of charging Lakotas. The second group, most of them unmounted now, formed a circle of sorts and tried to hold back the surging bands of Lakotas and Sahiyelas. Even one bunch of Arapahos was there, eager to avenge their brothers slain on Powder River.

For a time the snow-covered countryside was painted black by powder smoke. Among the soldiers were wasicuns with new, rapid-firing rifles. These guns cut down many warriors until there were no more bullets for them. The Lakota chiefs then drew their bands back from the hill. Most were used to fighting man against man on horseback, and charging a solid blue line was confusing. Now they sent great showers of arrows high up into the air so that they fell upon the wasicuns without mercy. Unfortunately, many arrows also fell among those warriors who rushed ahead of their brothers.

Finally, as the arrows thinned the ranks of the enemy, Hokala gave a shout.

"It's a good day to die!" he cried. "Who will follow me and kill the wasicuns?"

"No!" Tacante screamed even as he followed his friend up the hillside. Bullets split the air, splintered the branches of the nearby trees, kicked up fragments of rock, and smashed into bone, muscle, and vitals. Hokala stumbled as a bullet smashed his knee. A nearby Oglala was struck twice in the neck, and his head sagged to one side as he rolled down the hillside. Tacante felt a bullet tear through his war shirt. Another nicked the buffalo shield. Then the first wave of Lakotas was upon the soldiers.

The wild-eyed warriors slashed with knives and hacked with axes. The terrified bluecoats fell back in disorder, unhinging the whole line. Sahiyelas broke the circle on the other side, and now a fresh mass of Lakotas lent its force to the attack. In such close quarters, rifles and carbines were useless. Knives slashed, rifle butts clubbed, voices cursed in different tongues, and men died.

Tacante felt as a child, for though he had fought many times, he never knew such desperation. These wasicuns stood and fought with great courage. A few tried to get away, but it was impossible, and most knew it. Tacante drove his knife into one bluecoat's chest. Even as the blade cut the life from the soldier, he struggled to free his own knife from the grip of Tacante's left wrist.

A second wasicun ran about firing his empty pistol and wailing like a woman. No one would strike him down, for the Lakotas thought him touched. One after another of the soldiers died, but still this one crazy wasicun fired his empty gun. He was the last white face standing, and for a moment it seemed the Lakotas might let him go.

"You can't hurt me!" the wasicun cried as he flung his pistol aside and hurried to escape down the slope.

"Now we can kill him," a Sahiyela said, and they fell upon him without mercy. Tacante covered his ears to escape the hideous cries.

Only the wounded were left, and Tacante gazed at the bleeding soldiers with a heavy heart. These men had fought well. Many Indians were dead or wounded, though.

"Finish them!" one Lakota called.

"Leave them to my knife," a Sahiyela pleaded.

The Arapahos wasted no time. As they stripped bodies, they cut each so no whisper of life could remain.

Tacante took the scalps of the soldiers he had killed, then descended the hill to where Hokala lay. The Badger's knee was bound already, and he was complaining that he would miss out on the many fine things carried by the wasicuns on the hill.

"I'll see you have a rifle," Tacante promised. He then joined the others atop the hill.

Many good rifles and cartridges were there. Tacante collected three carbines and filled a small bag with lead and caps for his pistols. As he reached down to loosen a belt from a fallen wasicun, the soldier's eyes opened.

"I'll just be a minute dyin'," he said, wearily raising a small silver cross in one hand and mumbling to himself. "Go ahead with your work, friend. Wouldn't want them others to know."

"You would find my knife as sharp," Tacante growled as he unbuckled the belt.

"You got no belly for that, son," the wasicun said. "Seen you at the fort, I have. With Le Doux's boy."

"It makes me no less a Lakota," Tacante said, drawing his knife. But before the blade could strike, the air rushed out of the wasicun's lungs. The soldier's face sank into a soft layer of snow, and it appeared he was smiling.

"Maybe there is power in your cross," Tacante said as he placed the small bit of silver in the soldier's mouth. It would be hard to find there. Tacante then stripped the body of its heavy wool uniform, for such cloth would be hard to come by now, and Itunkala, his brother, would soon outgrow his shirts.

As with the wagon people, many of the soldiers were cut up. A man deprived of hands or with his hamstrings cut would be crippled on the other side. Thus many believed. The Sahiyelas cut pieces off men and put them in strange places. It seemed a great game to them. Tacante kept them away from the men he had killed.

"They fought bravely," Tacante said. "I marked them in the Lakota way. It is enough."

The Sahiyelas thought to argue, but the fire growing in Tacante's eyes sent them away.

"Collect the wounded and the dead," Sunkawakan Witkotkoke suggested, and Tacante slung his captured rifles onto one shoulder, hung his bow and shield on the other, and carried his bundle of clothing and cartridges down the hill. Cehupa Maza was waiting with the horses. His leg was bound, but blood continued to seep through the cloth bandages.

Tacante secured his booty to his horse, then helped Hokala up. Once Badger was mounted, the three young men raised a triumphant howl and bid farewell to the Horse. Sunka Sapa rode by to show the scalp he took, then wished them luck on their return.

"Watcher and I remain," he explained. "There are bluecoats yet eager to fall upon my knife."

Tacante gazed back up the hill. He thought of the white blanket that covered the naked wasicuns in his dream. Snow was sure to come soon, but even it could not conceal the terrible fight that had taken place there. Yes, it would be a remembered battle. No wasicun who visited that place and saw that sight could hunger for the same fate.

"Hau, we are warriors!" Hokala sang as his face twisted in pain.

"We fight the enemies of the people!" Cehupa Maza shouted.

"Brave hearts, sing loud," Tacante added, "for ours is a hard road."

"Ayyy!" the three friends howled as they turned their horses toward the distant lodges that would welcome them. It was a long way to ride in such difficult weather. Already snowflakes danced like feathers in the chill north wind. The white blanket of Tacante's dream was falling upon the dead. As for the living, well, they would have to provide their own.

"We should have taken a wasicun horse," Cehupa Maza complained. "Our people always need horses in winter."

"We have enough," Tacante muttered. "We are alive. And we have people whose hearts will warm when we return."

"Ayyy!" Hokala howled. "Fine scalps we bring! Our sisters will be proud."

Tacante glanced back at his companions. Each raised a strip of yellow-brown hair. He wondered how young warriors lamed by bullets could rush on to strike down the enemy. It was the great strength of the Lakota, he decided. And the folly, too, perhaps. Those rapid-shooting rifles had cut down many warriors. Where one gun appeared, others were certain to follow. Bows and lances could never stand against such weapons. And unlike the thunder guns, a rifle could be carried across deep ravines and up great mountains.

Chapter Eleven

The journey to Powder River proved to be a difficult one. Tacante and his wounded friends endured the sharp agonies of biting wind and numbing cold. Their horses grew weary, for there was only the yellow buffalo grasses dug from beneath powdery snow for the animals to eat.

Tacante also felt hunger's gnawing teeth. His food bag was nearly empty, and he gave the last of his wasna to Hokala. The Badger was hot with fever, and his knee festered. Tacante prayed they would soon be among the people. He Hopa would chase the evil odors from Hokala's leg.

Cehupa Maza's wound grew better. There wasn't any wasicun lead in the ankle, plaguing the healing spirits a man holds in his heart. The Jaw walked with a pronounced limp, wincing when he placed weight on the injured foot, but he refused to cry out or complain. And if Tacante set off on foot to shoot game for the spit, Cehupa Maza would follow.

They had but little success. Oh, once a small rabbit venturing out of its hole was shot, but its meat barely staved off the jaws of hunger. Tacante felt himself growing thinner. At night, when the three young Lakotas huddled in a makeshift shelter, they made a game of counting each other's ribs. And when Hokala lay shivering and moaning from the pain of his wound, Tacante spread his own threadbare blanket atop the Badger and prayed Powder River lay not far ahead.

Fortunately, the three skeletons rode their war ponies into Hinhan Hota's snowbound camp that next day. Hokala was slumped across the neck of his horse, and Tacante called for He Hopa, the wise old medicine man.

"His knee's been shattered," Tacante explained. "Will you use your power to make him one again?"

"Ah, I will try," the old one answered. "With your help."

Tacante gazed at the medicine man with solemn eyes and agreed. The young warrior then saw to his horse, presented the scalps to Wicatankala, and briefly greeted his father and young brother. Tacante spread the captured clothes beside his mother's place near the door of the lodge.

"These are good wool," he said, casting his eyes away from the woman's smiling face. "They will keep Itunkala warm in the coldest times. Perhaps someone will make him a shirt from them."

"I can make such a shirt," Tasiyagnunpa declared, taking the clothes. "I'll also make my first son a warrior shirt."

"He'd have use for it," Tacante replied.

It was a strange way to speak son to mother and mother to son, but it prevented the softness of a woman from smothering the warrior spirit in her son. Such was the Lakota way.

Tacante remained only another moment. His sister filled a platter with cold corn cakes and wasna, and he hungrily ate every scrap. Then, after smiling shyly toward Wicatankala, he hurried out into the cold. He Hopa had sought help. Soon it would be there.

Tacante had spent many hours learning the medicine herbs and the power of the chants. As he stood over Hokala and watched He Hopa open the festering wound, Tacante tried to recall every word of instruction. He Hopa noticed and smiled faintly.

"A man learns best what he does," the old man remarked, pointing toward a flint knife with a yellowing bone handle. It wasn't sharp like the fine steel blades the wasicun traders brought to the plains, but it was of the earth. He Hopa chanted as he cut Hokala's flesh. The Badger fought the pain, but still a groan passed his lips. Tacante held his friend firmly by the shoulders as He Hopa's knife cut deeper. Soon the medicine man drew out the pounded fragments of lead and small slivers of bone. After draining a yellow fluid, He Hopa called attention to the bright red blood which followed.

"Ah, the evil odors have fled," the old man explained. He then peppered the wound with a mixture of pounded buffalo horn and various curing herbs before binding the knee with wet buckskin. The binding would tighten, and the bleeding would stop.

"I will live?" Hokala asked when Tacante held a numbing drink to his friend's lips.

"If you keep from the path of wasicun bullets," Tacante answered. Hokala closed his eyes and allowed sleep to end the pain. Tacante then devoted himself to chanting prayers and undergoing such personal sacrifices as brought power into the hands of a medicine man.

He Hopa often drew his own blood to bring the healing powers into the medicine lodge. Tacante made himself a reflection to the old man, matching each cut and echoing every chant. He Hopa noticed.

"Always I've seen the power in you, Tonska," He Hopa said. "Now the knowledge has come into your heart. Yours in the sacred way. Hau! Remember what you have learned, for only the earth and sky live long. Soon I go to the other side."

Tacante sighed. He feared the day He Hopa no longer walked the land, for there was so much not yet understood.

As the cold grip of winter tightened on Powder River, Hokala grew stronger. Badger's was not a spirit to be kept abed, and though he walked with the use of a forked limb, he joined in brief hunts on days when the sun fought off the white haze.

Hokala Huste, he was now called. Limping Badger. It was a name spoken with honor, and the young ones were forever pleading for the tale of Hokala's fight with the wasicuns.

Tacante busied himself seeing to the needs of the horses or accompanying Hinhan Hota on rides to the other Lakota winter camps. There was also time to join He Hopa for medicine prayers. The best moments, though, were spent teaching Itunkala the skills of the hunt.

Mouse had now marked seven snows on the earth. It was fitting that this, his eighth winter, be a remembered time. So it was, for never did the wind howl so mournfully. All the world shivered under the daunting cold. But even so, Itunkala never flinched, for he was the son of Hinhan

Hota and the brother of Tacante, Buffalo Heart, a young man revered among the people for his many coups.

Tacante found great contentment in the admiring eyes of his small brother. Before, when the Mouse had been little more than a bundle of useless brown flesh, Tacante had despaired. Now the boy was alert and active. His feet carried him swiftly, like an antelope, and if small, his heart promised a future life marked by brave deeds and great devotion.

It was well Itunkala's company warmed the hard days of bitter winter, for the snows seemed reluctant to pass. Hunger plagued the camp, and only the fortunate killing of an occasional elk held off the perils of starvation. Even so, death came to the people. Two children caught fever and closed their eyes to the world of the earth-walkers. Then, while the popping moon waned, a wailing cry again filled the air. He Hopa was dead.

Not since the death of the other Tacante, he who was Ate, Father, had such a sense of loss descended. Then the boy Mastincala had been unable to help build the burial scaffold or prepare the body. Now, as an honored young man, Tacante rode to the neighboring camps to gather the medicine man's family.

Wanbli Cannunpa, the Eagle Pipe, arrived with his many daughters and two sons to oversee the mourning. It was Tacante, though, who helped Hehaka dress the body in finest robes. Much ceremony attended the erecting of a ghost lodge over the burial scaffold, and Hinhan Hota slew a fine war pony so that He Hopa might ride across the great unknown. Tacante himself hung the pony's tail on the burial scaffold.

Wanbli Cannunpa made such a feast as could be managed in those days of want and gave presents to honor his father-in-law. Finally the medicine man's belongings were packed away for the year remaining before the final mourning act, the giving up of the ghost ceremony in which those belongings would be handed to others.

Tacante faced a second sadness, as well. He Hopa's dying sent Hehaka back to her father's lodge. The deer woman had caught Tacante's eye more and more, and twice he had drawn her to his blanket so that they sat whispering warm words of the better days that would come with the summer sun.

"Wanbli Cannunpa," Tacante said as the honored warrior prepared to return to his people, "I will soon mark the end of my nineteenth snow walking the earth. I am a blooded warrior, a man of many horses, and

I would offer you three ponies to show my worthiness as a husband for Hehaka, your daughter."

"Ah, she is dear to my heart and too long absent from my lodge," Eagle Pipe answered. "Three ponies speaks of a generous heart, but you are young. Soon comes the buffalo hunt, and afterward the young men will ride again to fight the wasicuns. There is time for taking a wife later. Be patient, Tacante."

The rebuke stung him as a quirt upon the cheek might have felt. He backed away with sad eyes and left the Pipe to go upon his way.

As the snows finally started their thaw, Hinhan Hota began his preparations for the buffalo hunt. Tacante helped ready the ponies and make fresh arrows. But his heart was full of longing mixed with a growing bitterness. He pledged himself to fill the wasna pouches and strike down the enemies of the people.

Word will soon travel among the camps that I, Tacante, am a man to be followed. My lodge will be honored, and Wanbli Cannunpa will know his words were spoken with a foolish heart. I'm of an age to have a wife, am I not?

Tacante's eyes glowed with fiery determination, and Hinhan Hota noticed. When the scouts at last found a herd, the chief drew Tacante aside.

"My son, you will lead the young men," the Owl declared. "Take your party to the far side of the herd while I strike this."

"Hau, Ate," Tacante answered. "You will see I am worthy of your trust. Many buffalo will fall to my bow arm."

Another time such a boast might have been admonished, but Tacante spoke with the strong heart of a man determined to do as he said. When the Lakotas closed in on the grazing herd, Tacante proved it was so. He spread his companions in a thin line, then led the charge that broke the herd.

As a small one, Tacante's arm had lacked the strength to match the bow arms of his fellows. Now he showed what changes could come upon a man tormented by rejection. Each time Tacante notched an arrow, he drove his horse close to the stampeding buffalo so that he could fire behind the shoulder and deep into the animal's heart. First one bull, then another, and another again pitched forward in death. Five arrows Tacante fired. Five buffalo fell.

"Hau! He is first among us!" Cehupa Maza called as the young men collected around the eight animals they slew.

"He is brother to Tatanka," Hokala Huste claimed.

Even Hinhan Hota was surprised to hear of such success. And when the people feasted on the tasty hump meat, they spoke proudly of how the boy born to them as Mastincala had proven his was the true heart of the people. He'd fought well at the battle of the hundred slain, and he was a proven hunter. Tacante was a man to follow.

Chapter Twelve

Following the success of the spring buffalo hunt, Tacante turned his thoughts once again to the wasicuns traveling the stolen road and the soldiers in their walled forts. Waawanyanka and Sunka Sapa had stayed that bitter winter, watching the bluecoats at the middle fort. Now, with the sun shining again, they came to visit their relatives.

"New soldiers have come," Sunka Sapa told Tacante. "Wagons move through the heart of our good hunting lands. Who will fight them? Sunkawakan Witkotkoke calls for the young men to return. He said that I should say to you that the brave hearts must lead. Will you come?"

Tacante glanced around him. Those days had been good. He had raced his horse against the neighboring bands of Oglalas and Sihasapas, winning every time. Often he walked out into the hills with Itunkala, teaching his brother how to track game, to shoot the large bow, and even which herbs could heal wounds or ease the stomach's pains. Still the sting of Wanbli Cannunpa's refusal scarred his heart, though. Tacante knew the Pipe would look favorably upon a young warrior who rode into battle with the Oglala's strange one.

"I'll come," Tacante said.

And so the Heart followed his two friends back to the Big Horns.

With them came Cehupa Maza and a mended Hokala. Though both of the wounded Sicangus suffered from the hard riding, they never complained. For war was a young man's duty, and no Lakota hid when the call came to take the hard path.

The five young men joined Sunkawakan Witkotkoke near where the stolen road passed the hill of the hundred slain. Crazy Horse welcomed them warmly. He and his Oglalas prepared a feast, and all filled their bellies. Then the horse spoke of a band of wasicuns stealing their way by darkness north toward Yellowstone River.

"These thieves who would steal our land walk in the shadows, thinking they are smart. Tomorrow we will punish them greatly,"

"Hau!" Hokala shouted. "They will die hard."

"I will strike them down," Sunka Sapa added.

"Ah, each thing in its time," Sunkawakan Witkotkoke replied. "We leave at first light. They have many good guns, and the danger is great. Be invisible to their eyes and ears, Lakotas. Let's stalk them as our fathers taught us to trail the deer. Use the bow. Let your silent arrows kill these thieves as the thunderbolts might."

The Lakotas whooped their agreement. Then the warriors took to their beds, for morning would begin early.

Tacante passed a rather restless night. He wrapped himself in a heavy buffalo hide, but still a chill wind blended with the moist, damp ground to send spasms of cold through his weary frame. Nearby the other young men suffered, too. A pair of Oglala boys brought along to tend to the ponies shivered with misery. To make matters worse, a flurry of snow greeted the dawn.

"Winter's come again," Hokala complained as he tried to straighten his stiff leg.

"It's a bad sign," Waawanyanka added. "Our medicine has gone bad."

"When has snow been a bad sign?" Cehupa Maza asked. "The world was white as moonlight when we slew the hundred wasicuns. Hau! We will kill these others, too."

Hokala continued to argue, but the others took Cehupa Maza's good words to heart. All the young men hungered for battle. Some had never counted coup, and others hoped to take some of the new rifles the wasicun travelers carried.

"Come," Sunkawakan Witkotkoke spoke as he appeared among his followers. "It's time to fight."

"Hau!" the young men answered. "It's a good day to die"

"Better we should live," the Horse said, drawing them close. "Here's how it can be done."

Tacante listened attentively. It was a simple plan, but it should work. Sunkawakan Witkotkoke and the Oglalas would encircle the wasicuns on one side, and Tacante and his Sicangu companions would close the gap from the other direction. The Lakotas would wait for the wasicuns to light their cook fires. That would be the signal to attack. If all the warriors moved suddenly and with determination, the fight would surely be a short one, and no Lakota would be hurt. The warriors didn't fear death themselves, but the loss of a friend or relative cast shadows over any personal glory. Better all should survive. That was the best kind of victory, Tacante knew.

The Indians set off alone or in pairs toward the wasicun camp. These thieves traveled on horseback. They brought no wagons, no band of women and little ones to slow their movements. As Tacante approached the circle of blankets, he saw two wasicuns stacking sticks to make a fire. Another one mixed flour in a bowl. It was strange to see white men cooking, for always it seemed they brought women along to do such work. These wasicuns weren't the lazy kind Tacante had known at Fort Laramie. They also kept a guard, for two of them stood together atop a rocky hill overlooking the camp. The other two wasicuns remained in their blankets.

Ah, it was a good moment to strike, Tacante told himself. If only the fire builders would strike a spark! But in spite of two tries, the spark wouldn't fly from the small flint onto the dry grass spread over the kindling twigs. Finally, after issuing a string of curses, one of the wasicuns managed to light the fire.

"Best get the skillet greased, Tom" one of the fire builders said. "I'm hungry."

He wouldn't be for long. Two arrows flew out of the nearby trees. Both struck the hungry fire builder in the back, and he fell forward, smothering the fire.

"Lord, it's Indians!" the cook yelled.

Before a second alarm could stir the camp, the Lakotas charged.

Knives and hatchets cut and slashed, and the four remaining wasicuns in the camp fell in the same instant. The two guards fired their rifles wildly and retreated to a wall of boulders.

Tacante had observed the attack, but he had been a step slow rushing the camp. He now followed the Horse up the hill, then crawled along the rock wall. Just on the other side of those stones were two wasicuns armed with rifles. A false move meant death. But when Sunkawakan Witkotkoke hurled himself over the wall and plunged his blade into the first guard, Tacante jumped the second. The wasicun managed to slap the knife away, but Tacante had separated the guard from his rifle. For a moment the two of them rolled across the hard ground, grappling for the knife. Then the wasicun gripped a rock and slammed it against Tacante's chest. The young Sicangu rolled away, momentarily stunned. The guard picked up the knife and shouted triumphantly. But when he pounced, Tacante jumped away, and the drawn knife struck only rock.

Tacante now pinned the wasicun's arms and dug a knee into the intruder's back. The white man screamed in pain.

"Your friends are all dead," Tacante told the wasicun. "See how Wakan Tanka punishes those who cross our country, stealing the game which feeds the hungry children in winter."

The wasicun strained to twist his head around to look at the man who held his life, who was lecturing him in his own language. Tacante's voice was ghostly, haunting, and he saw the terrifying effect it had.

"Don't finish him," Sunka Sapa suggested. "Leave him for the Sahiyelas."

The wasicun must have understood the Lakota word for the tribe he knew as Cheyenne. He shouted loudly and shook one arm free. But before he could escape, Tacante forced his victim's face into the ground. The wasicun struggled vainly. Tacante recalled the cutting done on the spectacled wagon boy and felt a chill grip his insides. He took his knife and made a single quick thrust into the wasicun's vitals. There was a gasp, and then the life went out of him.

"Hau!" Hokala howled, showing off the scalp he had earlier taken.

"Hau!" Tacante echoed as he cut a square of hair from the wasicun's scalp. He then took a cartridge belt, a small pouch of gold coins, and the wasicun's fine new rifle. Waawanyanka stripped the rest of the clothing, for all the people were in want. After collecting every useful piece of equipment, the Lakotas gathered the seven wasicun horses, together with ten pack mules, and headed back to the warrior camp near the middle fort.

Such fights proved the value of a good plan. Not all raids ended with such success. Many of the wasicun wagon parties now carried the many-firing Winchester rifles, and ten men so armed were as good as a bluecoat army. Other times some young warrior riding to his first fight would give away the trap and expose his companions to murderous rifle fire.

The Lakotas continued to make the wasicun travelers pay a dear toll for crossing Powder River, though. Warriors died, but so did the wagon people. As for the bluecoats, the woodcutters and supply trains suffered worst. But by late summer the soldier chiefs had grown smarter. Now the woodcutters went in large bands, and cavalry never left them undefended.

Mahpiya Luta took note. These wasicuns were no longer fools. They fired often at the decoys, but now they never followed into the jaws of a Lakota trap. The fort was too strong to attack. Only the woodcutters remained vulnerable. So it was decided to attack the next group that ventured beyond the shadow of the fort's walls.

The opportunity was not long in arriving, for the wasicuns needed wood for cooking. They sent a party out early in the morning, and Tacante was among the hundreds of Lakotas who followed Mahpiya Luta to a grassy clearing encircled by fourteen wagon boxes. The wheels were being used to move logs. The boxes had been used for a horse corral.

The woodcutters had formed a train of these log-carrying wheels and started for the fort. It was the chance Mahpiya Luta had hoped for. He motioned toward the log people.

"Hau!" a band of young Oglalas shouted. In an instant the young men rode down on the woodcutters. They cut the mules from their harnesses and drove the animals off in triumph.

The rest of the warriors guarded the trail in hopes the bluecoats might try to get their animals back. They didn't. Now the woodcutters hurried from the pines to the box corral. Some had seen the many Lakotas and spread the alarm. Surrounded in the open, with no mounts, they must certainly perish.

"Look!" came a cry. "Wagons!"

Mahpiya Luta beheld a train coming from the fort. Instantly a band of warriors charged, and the wagon soldiers turned and desperately fought their way back to the protection of the fort. Now there were only the woodcutters to finish.

"Hau!" Hokala shouted as he raced ahead of Tacante to join a band of Sihasapas. Tacante glanced around until he saw Sunkawakan Witkotkoke. Crazy Horse stood beside his pony, hurriedly painting his hailstone medicine on his chest. Tacante held his captured rifle high in one hand and urged the Horse to lead the fight.

"Come!" Hokala screamed from the direction of the boxes.

"Tacante," Cehupa Maza pleaded. "We must go!"

Tacante saw Sunka Sapa join Hokala. Now there could be no more waiting. Already the first warriors were closing in on the wagon boxes. He could not delay. His place was with his brother Sicangus.

Waawanyanka arrived moments after Tacante, and the five friends howled fearlessly as they whipped their ponies into motion. The wasicuns were hiding in the boxes or behind sacks of supplies or oxen yokes. It mattered little. Tacante had often jumped his pony over taller objects than a wasicun wagon box, and the thin-skinned boxes had no power to hold back a bullet.

"Hau!" the warriors cried as they charged. "It's a good day to die!" And then, as if thunder had split the heavens, the wasicun bullets struck the charge.

Two Sihasapas were the first to fall. Then a young Oglala's horse went down. Waawanyanka's pony fell, too, and the Watcher only barely avoided being trampled.

Tacante turned away and hurried to where Waawanyanka stood helplessly watching bullets tear at the nearby earth.

"Hau, Waawanyanka!" Tacante shouted as he raced by. The Watcher managed to grab Tacante's extended hand and pull himself up behind him. A howl of approval followed the rescue.

The attack against the boxes was going badly, though. The Lakotas had failed to penetrate the circle, and now the warriors raced back and forth firing arrows and bullets toward the boxes. Their hidden enemies returned the fire, striking down horses and riders. Even when the Lakotas hung off the sides of their mounts, wasicun bullets could find their ponies. Drawing fire might work if others were preparing to charge from another side, but most of the warriors collected on the nearby hills and watched the murder.

Sunkawakan Witkotkoke then appeared. His was a skill unseen in others, for his power was great to inspire the young men. He called out his war cry and urged a fresh attack.

"Ride hard at the wasicuns," he said. "Then stop and let them shoot. They will stop their shooting and reload. Then we will strike."

Tacante left Waawanyanka safely out of rifle range before turning to follow the Horse. There was a great feeling among the young men. The Horse had thought of a good plan, and the young Oglalas and Sicangus had the courage to follow it.

The plan didn't work, though. First the wasicuns shot many of the lead warriors. The survivors waited for the shooting to halt, but it never did. A steady torrent of bullets struck down one after another of the brave hearts.

Perhaps it was because the Lakotas boasted too often of their power that the medicine went bad. Or maybe it was only another of the hard things the spirits set out to make the warriors strong. Tacante never knew. He did get close enough to the boxes before his pony was shot to notice a strange thing. The wasicuns had new rifles that could be loaded lying down. The bluecoats fired, then reloaded, and fired again so swiftly there was no opportunity to charge unharmed.

Tacante huddled behind his dead horse and fired the new rifle at the boxes. Once he thought he must have struck a bluecoat, but he couldn't be certain. He had lost heart. The wonderful buffalo shield was pierced a dozen times that day, and all around him brave young men bled to death.

Gradually the Lakotas gave up the charges and withdrew out of range. Tacante, too, fell back. He cautiously wove his way between fallen horses until he reached the safety of the sloping hill. There he joined other Lakota riflemen who were continuing the fight. A few others fired burning arrows at the wagons, but though they caused much smoke and burned some of the wagons, the woodcutters remained safe.

One final attack was planned. There was a ravine which led to the wagon box, and a party of young men agreed to try a charge on foot. Many horses had already been lost, for the wagons blocked the path too well. Men could rush the boxes, leap over their sides, and overwhelm the wasicuns inside.

"Hau!" Tacante yelled. "Surely we will succeed this time."

He stood with Hokala and Cehupa Maza on either side. Sunka Sapa and Waawanyanka rushed over to join. Again the five friends would fight together. Tacante made a strong medicine prayer and lifted his riddled shield skyward in hopes of gaining protection for them all. Then they joined the hundred warriors in the ravine.

A wild, reckless charge might well have succeeded. But the ground was rough, and the last steps between the ravine and the wagons were full of slain horses and fallen men. The rifle fire was hot as ever. No sooner did Tacante take a step in the open than he felt something warm splatter his bare shoulder. He gazed in horror as Cehupa Maza, the fearless Iron Jaw, fell forward. His face was blown apart, and two red circles marked his chest.

"Wakan Tanka, give me strength," Tacante prayed as he struggled to grip his rifle. A wasicun bullet then shattered the stock, and a second pierced his chest just above the left nipple and left through the armpit. He dropped to his knees, then screamed in rage.

"Tacante!" Hokala called. The Badger turned back, only to be struck in the right shoulder.

So, here is where the young men of the Sicangu will die, Tacante thought as he discarded his fine new rifle, its stock shattered and the magazine hopelessly fouled. He drew a pistol and fired off its six rounds. By then the attack was clearly coming apart. The whole wasicun band was firing into the shattered remains of the chargers.

"Where are the others?" Hokala asked as he crawled to Tacante's side.

"Cehupa Maza is dead," Tacante whispered.

"The warriors," Hokala cried. "The older men. Why don't they join us?"

"Enough have died already," Tacante answered. "It's a bad day for the Lakotas."

"Yes," Hokala agreed as he stared at the blood seeping from Tacante's chest.

"Once my father, Hinhan Hota, said that a man knows nothing of his birth," Tacante recounted. "It's only for him to die well."

"Yes," Hokala agreed. "Can you stand?"

Tacante tried to rise, but strong hands reached out and pulled him to the ground.

"It's too good a day to die," Waawanyanka declared. "Have heart, Tacante. We've come to take you back."

Sunka Sapa then knelt beside Hokala, allowing the Badger to climb onto his back. Tacante sighed as Watcher slipped an arm under his arm and helped him crawl from the bloody grass. A step at a time, they withdrew down the ravine until the four of them sat together in the pines.

"I'll bring back the Jaw now," Sunka Sapa said, heading back toward the ravine as Waawanyanka tore a blanket into strips for bindings.

"I owe you my life," Tacante told his friend.

"I owed you mine," Waawanyanka answered. "We're brothers now, yes?"

"Always," Tacante agreed, gripping the Watcher's hand firmly. "And more. My kola, Waawanyanka."

"Yes," Watcher agreed.

"And you, Hokala?" Tacante asked.

"Yes," Hokala readily answered.

And when Sunka Sapa returned, a fourth firm hand was added to the pledge.

The four kolas headed south toward Hinhan Hota's camp that afternoon, riding captured wasicun mules. The animals were proof of the poor bargain they had made. Exchanging blood and fine war ponies for a hundred overworked mules! Behind them the smoke from burning wagon boxes mixed with the roar of a thunder gun to mark the scene of the terrible fight. They needed no reminders, though. Tied to Sunka Sapa's horse, the sole surviving pony, were the bloody remains of Cehupa Maza, their true friend.

You are the first, Tacante thought as he bounced painfully along atop the mule's bare back. But not the last, he feared.

Chapter Thirteen

Tacante led the weary young Lakotas into Hinhan Hota's camp. The hollow cheeks and bent, bloodied bodies of the four warriors quickly silenced the brave heart shouts of the old men. Little Itunkala raced out to take his brother's horse, and Tacante let the boy tend the broad-backed mule.

"You are hurt," Itunkala called in surprise.

"Yes," Tacante admitted, touching his brother's shoulder, "I and the others."

A throng soon gathered to gaze at the frozen eyes of Cehupa Maza. Voices cried out, and the women trilled the mourning chant. Hinhan Hota greeted his son with sad, knowing eyes, and Tacante collapsed in his father's powerful arms.

"Look to Hokala," Tacante managed to mumble before darkness swallowed him.

In the days that followed, Tacante told the Owl of the wagon-box fight. Hinhan Hota took in every word, then put on a dark face.

"Wakan Tanka makes our path hard," the chief said solemnly. "But we have brave hearts."

Tacante drank in the words, but they failed to cheer him. A brave heart had not saved Cehupa Maza. Iron Jaw was dead. The bullet that had torn through Tacante's left side left him sore and mostly useless. Hokala remained in bed. So it was with every band among the warring Lakotas.

Flesh mended, though, and before the first snows fell on the earth that winter, Tacante was again riding to the hunt. Hokala's shoulder remained stiff, and his limp was more pronounced than ever. Still, the boys of the camp tended his needs and sang the brave songs of his many fights.

Great honor soon fell upon the four young kolas. In the dead of night, a drum awoke the camp. Tacante tossed off his blankets and threw on clothes. The memory of Blue Creek was suddenly with him, and he feared the wasicuns had come. The drum raised no alarm, however. For already assembled in the center of camp were the many members of the Kit-foxes, the famed warrior society known for the many brave hearts it sent into battle.

Hinhan Hota, who was one of the two leaders of the Kit-foxes, then looked to old Wahacanka Mazasu, the Bullet Shield. The Shield was a pipe carrier, one of the honored two who presided over the society's meetings. Wahacanka Mazasu called forth Tacante to join the Tokalas, the Foxes, and the young man stepped to his father's side. Hokala was summoned next. Finally Waawanyanka and Sunka Sapa were called.

The four young men were led away to a secret place. There older warriors recounted their many coups. Howls of approval followed. Then a fire was kindled, and the pipe carriers invoked the spirits to look upon the company with favor. Finally the young men were placed between two lines of their elders and forced to walk calmly as one after another of the older warriors jabbed lances or knives at the unprotected flesh of the novices. Tacante read the fierce eyes of the Tokalas, but he refused to fill his heart with fear. Even when a knife drew blood and a lance pricked his tender shoulder, he didn't cry out. He grinned as he saw his companions also complete the difficult task.

Afterward many medicine words were spoken, and the song of the Tokalas was sung. It was a good song, boasting of courage and determination. When the older warriors finished, Tacante and his friends sang it.

"I am a fox. I'm supposed to die. If there's anything that's difficult, anything dangerous, that's mine to do."

When the words died down, the second pipe carrier, Wicahpi Inyan, the Stone Star, recounted brave heart deeds performed by the Kit-foxes in fights against the Crows and the Snakes.

"Now you are with us, my sons," Hinhan Hota told the new foxes at last. "Much is expected of a Tokala. Much."

The two lance bearers, Wamanon, the Robber, and Tonweya, Rides Ahead, stood silently and showed their lances. Throughout the Lakota people there was no braver man than a lance bearer. Tacante knew that once such a man drove that lance in the earth, tied its cord to his leg, and faced the enemy, he could not retreat with honor. Only another Tokala could free a lance bearer of his obligation, and that was rarely done. Such warriors carried their lances but a short time when the people were at war.

"One day, if you prove your heart is brave, you may come to carry the lance," Wamanon explained.

"Hau!" the others shouted.

The Tokalas then welcomed their new companions with food and good talk. Tacante felt himself glowing in the bright gaze of his father's eyes.

"A man can only be proud of such a son," Hinhan Hota said, gripping Tacante's wrists.

Hinhan Hota moved the people north as winter arrived. He joined his camp to that of Wanbli Cannunpa's Oglalas and a smaller band of Sahiyelas. Nearby, Tacante was pleased to learn, a larger Oglala camp nestled among the tall pines. It was there that Sunkawakan Witkotkoke erected his winter lodge. The Horse soon appeared to greet his young admirers.

"Hau! All the brave young men aren't dead," Sunkawakan Witkotkoke shouted.

"See how the scars boast of courage," Sunka Sapa cried as he opened Tacante's shirt and revealed the scars where the bullet had entered and left. Hokala displayed his shoulder, too, and the Horse shouted again.

"Soon we will kill all the wasicuns," he boasted. "Brave hearts! We will punish them for the wagon box."

Tacante found himself howling in response. Afterward, as he recalled the pain, saw again the cold, lifeless eyes of Iron Jaw, he had less eagerness to ride again to war. And as the heavens emptied and the snows painted the land white and solemn, even the bravest warriors ceased to speak of battle. It was enough to see the people had wood to burn and meat to eat.

Tacante devoted most of his time to hunting. The wasicun wagons traveling the stolen road had run much of the game into the hills, but a clever man could still locate an elk or a few deer. Often Tacante returned with fresh meat for the kettles and hides for his mother and sister to work. Whenever the fierce bite of the cold north wind abated, he took little Itunkala out to shoot rabbits or look after the horses. And when the sun broke through the haze under the tree-popping moon, he took his courting flute to Wanbli Cannunpa's lodge and waited with his blanket for Hehaka, the Deer Woman.

As a blooded warrior who now wore the feathers of many coups in his hair, Tacante was received more cheerfully by old Eagle Pipe. Now the two were both Tokalas. And when the Oglalas spoke of their battles, young Tacante's name was often mentioned.

Still Wanbli Cannunpa held back permission for Hehaka to be a wife. The girl had become a healer among the Oglalas, a medicine woman. Old He Hopa had been a man of great power, and the Pipe hoped his daughter might possess some of the magic. But though Hehaka knew of the medicine plants and could pound the many powders, she did not know Wakan Tanka. Her dreams did not point the way.

"My father is disappointed," Hehaka told Tacante as they huddled beneath his blanket. "Soon he will see it is you that He Hopa guided upon the sacred path. When you next bring ponies, Wanbli Cannunpa will welcome you to his lodge."

Tacante hoped it would be so, but he saw no sign of it. It was another false promise, like the one spoken to the Oglalas by the wasicuns at the middle fort. One of the soldier chiefs, a man called Dandy, had talked of leaving the forts if the Lakotas would cease their attacks.

"If the wasicuns kept promises, no forts would have been built," Sunkawakan Witkotkoke said. It was what many thought. And when the bluecoats cut more wood to keep them warm when the heavy snows came, Dandy's words were seen for what they were, smoke in the wind.

Tacante was called to fight only once that winter. Wamanon, the Robber, spotted some wasicun horses under a light guard near where the woodcutters were working.

"I am a fox," Robber spoke. "Tokalas, follow me."

Soon a band formed. Tacante and Hokala rode with Hinhan Hota. Waawanyanka and Sunka Sapa were watching the bluecoats at middle fort.

At first it seemed an easy thing to do. The horses were digging their noses in the snow, then chewing the moist grass underneath. Only two wasicuns kept watch. Wamanon crept over and cracked the first one over the head with a rock. Hinhan Hota drove an arrow through the second one's chest. Both guards died silently, and the Lakotas collected the horses and prepared to drive them back to their camp. Then the air was torn by the blast of a soldier horn, and fifteen bluecoats galloped toward the startled horse stealers.

"Go, my brothers!" Wamanon shouted, planting his lance in the earth and binding his leg. "I'm a fox. I'm supposed to die."

Tacante didn't hear the rest of the brave heat song. He was too busy driving the wasicun ponies out past the river. Hokala turned and went to help the Robber, and others prepared to follow.

"It's for Wamanon to stay," Hinhan Hota explained.

"I can't let Hokala go alone, Ate," Tacante said as he climbed atop his horse. "We are kolas."

"Go, my brave heart son," the Owl said reluctantly. "Sting the wasicuns with your arrows."

Tacante howled and raced to where Wamanon stood waiting for the cavalry charge. The bluecoats roared out of a powdery white cloud, and they reached Robber before Hokala or Tacante got near. Guns barked, and the lance carrier was swallowed by violent death. Tacante and Hokala notched arrows and sent them flying among the wasicuns. One bluecoat screamed out in pain as an arrow found his hip, and another tumbled from his slain horse. Then ten bluecoats charged out of the snow.

"Tacante" Hokala called, glancing nervously at the onrushing horsemen.

"Only death waits here," Tacante said, letting fly a final arrow. "We must go."

The two young Lakotas then turned their horses into the pines and vanished, leaving the bluecoats to search fruitlessly most of the afternoon. Toward nightfall Tacante and Hokala returned to recover the slain Wamanon's body. For once the bluecoats had shown respect for a brave heart. They had taken Robber's elk-hide robe and his buckskin leggings, but they had covered him with a red blanket. The lance remained even now anchored in the snowy hillside.

"Hau, Wamanon!" Hokala shouted. "Yours was a brave heart death."

"Yes," Tacante agreed as they tied the stiff corpse atop Hokala's horse. The Badger then climbed up behind Tacante, and the two young friends returned to the camp, leading the second pony with its grim burden.

All the people mourned the fallen Robber. For three days the people grieved. Wamanon was placed on a scaffold in the high rocks, and songs were sung about his courage. The pipe carriers called the Tokalas together then, for a new lance bearer was needed. Tacante watched nervously as many eyes fell on his chest. It was a hard thing, staying behind to die. Tatanka, Bull Buffalo, had called upon him to live for the people.

Perhaps the Tokalas read the reluctance in Tacante's eyes, or perhaps they saw the concern written on Hinhan Hota's face. Maybe the pipe carriers, close as they were to Wakan Tanka, understood the Great Mystery and followed its urging. They sought out Hokala and placed the lance in his hands.

"Hokala Huste," Wicahpi Inyan said solemnly, "we of the Tokalas call upon you to bear the lance."

"Will you accept it, knowing the grave responsibilities that are given to a Tokala lance bearer?" Wahacanka Mazasu asked.

"I'm a fox," Hokala said gravely. "It's for me to do what is dangerous and difficult."

"Hau!" the others shouted. Tacante howled, even though inside he was scolding the weakness that made him glad it was Hokala who was called to bear the lance. Tacante saw the Badger dead that very moment, knew long life had been snatched from a brother who had never held back when Tacante faced danger.

Hokala gave many presents away, and Tacante honored his friend by giving two of the stolen wasicun horses to families whose animals had died of the harsh weather.

"I was certain they would give you the lance, Tacante," Hokala told his friend later. "It's you that's so often led the charge."

"It was you turned back to help Wamanon," Tacante said, driving the truth from his face. "They all saw."

Hokala glowed with pride, but Tacante only swallowed his own misery. The day Hokala first planted the lance and remained behind, Tacante swore to stay also. Perhaps that vow might ease his guilt.

He doubted it.

Winter soon brought another ceremony. A year had passed since the passing of old He Hopa, and Four Horns's family now brought out the many possessions of the medicine man and spread them in the snow.

"Hear us, friends," Wanbli Cannunpa called. "He who was called He Hopa is no more. We give up his ghost that he may walk in peace on the other side."

Hehaka and her sisters carried kettles and blankets to one family or another. Many fine shirts were given away to those in need. Buffalo hides and beaded moccasins were passed among the elders. Finally Wanbli Cannunpa lifted a fine medicine bonnet skyward. The buffalo horns protruding from each side had been a source of great power, and suddenly a great quiet settled over the camp.

"Wakan Tanka, bring power and wisdom to the man who wears this bonnet," Wanbli Cannunpa prayed. He then carried the medicine bonnet to Tacante and set it upon the startled young man's head.

"I'm not worthy," Tacante objected.

"He Hopa chose you," the Pipe explained. "His medicine charms are in my lodge, as are many powders. Who would know what to do with them? It's your heart Tatanka speaks to. Yours is the healing way."

Tacante dipped his head in modest submission, and the people howled their approval.

"I have no good horse to ride," Wanbli Cannunpa then added. "Perhaps you know of one I might like?"

"I do," Tacante said. "You know of the fine buckskin mare I have ridden to hunt the buffalo."

"Ah, such a fine gift would need to be answered. Is there something I have you could use?"

"Something of great value," Tacante answered, shyly shifting his eyes toward Hehaka.

"You have a dark horse, too, taken from the wasicuns."

"And a raven-colored stallion. These I would offer."

"Then come to my lodge when the sun rises," Wanbli Cannunpa said, gripping Tacante's wrists. "My daughter's heart will soar with the hawks."

"As mine will," Tacante said.

So it was that Tacante walked from the lodge of his father and took a wife. As was the custom, Tacante now adopted Hehaka's people as his own. He bid farewell to his Sicangu brothers, for now Wanbli Cannunpa would point the way. But scarcely had word been sent to the neighboring camps of the wedding feast when the scouts brought word that peace speakers had again come to Fort Laramie.

"Ah, the wasicuns speak often of peace," Mahpiya Luta spoke to a gathering of Oglalas. "If they want peace, they only have to leave our country and keep the thieves from Powder River."

Others spoke much the same, but Louis Le Doux arrived to say there were, indeed, two star chiefs and many other wasicuns at the fort. They brought presents and spoke of ending the killing.

"It's good word I bring," Louis told Tacante. "I'm pleased, too, that I'll be here to share your wedding feast."

"Yes," Tacante said, smiling at his brother-friend. "It's been a long time since we hunted elk. You, too, must soon find a wife. A trader's son has many good things to trade, and we have many women and not so many young men."

"We're not so young as when we watched Itunkala in his cradleboard. He's grown. You have, too."

"Yes," Tacante said, touching the fine black hairs that now spread beneath Hinkpila's nose. It was strange, this hairy face that had come to his brother-friend. "And you, Hinkpila."

"You'll come to the fort soon? Hinhan Hota, our father, has agreed to hear the peace speakers' words."

"Soon I will be Oglala," Tacante said, turning to look at Eagle Pipe. "Mahpiya Luta stays. Sunkawakan Witkotkoke stays. I, too, will remain until the soldiers leave."

"Then perhaps our paths will meet when summer returns," Louis said. "I will watch our brother."

"Yes," Tacante said sadly. "Itunkala is young. He's not lived among the wasicuns."

The two of them gripped each other's hands. Then Tacante went to seek out his father and brother.

"You go to the fort, Ate," Tacante said when he joined Hinhan Hota. "The Oglalas stay."

"Many stay," Hinhan Hota replied. "Some go. You've chosen well, my son. Be a good husband. Bring no dishonor on your family."

"I'd sooner die," Tacante assured his father. "You will say to my mother and sister that I thank them for the many fine presents they have made for me and my wife."

"It gives them pleasure to do it. You've been a good son and a worthy brother."

"Now I must talk with Itunkala."

"He waits for you even now," Hinhan Hota said, pointing to where the Mouse stood holding the patched buffalo shield.

Tacante led the boy across the snow-covered hillside. Itunkala had now passed eight winters upon the earth, and the beginnings of the man he would be were upon him. He was small, but his feet carried him swiftly, and his strong little arms made him a fair match for his bigger companions in the wrestling games favored by Lakota boys.

"I'll miss you on the hunt, Misun," Tacante said, using the favored word for his younger brother. His only blood brother.

"You promised to make me a bow of good ash," Itunkala said, resting his head against his brother's side.

"I'll do it. We won't be so long from each other's sight. Soon this war will be finished, and we will hunt the buffalo."

"You'll come to the fort?"

"When the fighting's done. Now Hinkpila, our brother, will look after you. He has many brothers, and he knows much. He'll show you strange things and teach you difficult words spoken by the wasicuns."

"I don't want to know such things!" Itunkala answered angrily. "The wasicuns kill our people. A wasicun put the hole in your side."

"Don't close your mind to what can be learned, Misun. A clever Lakota knows his enemies. He learns their weaknesses and turns that knowledge against them."

"Hau!" Itunkala shouted. "That's true."

"Come now with me to the wedding feast. Hehaka has no young brothers, and she wishes to see what one looks like. You'll sit beside me in a place of honor, and you can choose the best pieces of meat."

Itunkala grinned broadly, and the two of them walked together to where Hehaka's Oglala relations had erected the new lodge she would now share with her husband. Food was spread out on blankets, and already a crowd was gathering. It was only when the two brothers came near that Itunkala wavered. Clutching Tacante's hand, the Mouse tried not to let his sadness show. But the boy's feelings overwhelmed him, and Tacante lifted the boy onto one shoulder and walked on to greet his new wife and her family.

"Hau!" Wanbli Cannunpa cried. "I welcome my son, Tacante, to his new lodge."

Tacante responded with proud words, and then the people celebrated the union with much good food. Presents were given away freely, and there was singing and dancing. Later, when Tacante and Hehaka closed the buffalo-hide flap over their tipi's oval door and crept to the warm fire, they exchanged shy glances.

"Here I am for you, my husband," Hehaka said, baring herself.

"And I for you, lovely one," Tacante said as he peeled off his shirt.

Tacante felt an icy chill creep down his back as he loosened his leggings. Then Hehaka spread apart the rich buffalo hides her sisters had prepared for them. She lay on one side, watching with eager eyes as he removed his breechclout. She then grinned shyly as he joined her.

Tacante remembered the terrifying loneliness he'd felt at Blue Creek. Since that day he'd never known the perfect belonging he'd experienced as a small boy in his father's lodge. Now, as Hehaka drew him to her, that belonging returned. Every inch of him glowed with rare warmth, and he knew the great contentment that being one with another could bring.

No thoughts of fighting wasicuns or signing treaties invaded has mind that night. There was only Hehaka.

106

Chapter Fourteen

The wasicuns called it Red Cloud's War. Perhaps it was, for of all the chiefs and warriors determined to save Powder River and the last of the great hunting grounds, Mahpiya Luta's voice rose loudest. Even as the many Lakota and Sahiyela chiefs touched the pen to a new treaty at Fort Laramie, the Cloud, Sunkawakan Witkotkoke, and many other Lakotas remained in the Big Horn country, watching the bluecoats in their forts and raiding the wasicuns traveling the stolen road.

"Come to the fort and make peace," many voices urged. "See how the wasicuns reward us with their many presents. We have new guns that shoot far and fire many times. Hau! The hunting is good, and our young men will live to see many summers."

"So long as the wasicuns stay in this country, I will fight," Mahpiya Luta always answered. And many stayed with him.

Wanbli Cannunpa remained, and Tacante now followed his father-in-law. The heart longed to hear the wise, familiar voice of Hinhan Hota, and he missed the admiring eyes of little Itunkala. But Hehaka comforted him with her soft words and warm touch, and he enjoyed a new contentment.

Often he rode to the watching hill to share time with Waawanyanka and Sunka Sapa. The two young men would sometimes return to Eagle

Pipe's camp and enjoy the chief's hospitality. Hehaka often eased the pain of many days in the saddle with her healing herbs, and she was equally gifted preparing fry bread or stewing buffalo and elk meat.

"Ah, it's a good bargain you made, Tacante," Sunka Sapa remarked. "You've found a wife to fatten your belly and heal your hurts."

"And one with a pleasing face as well," Waawanyanka added. "As for fat, she seems well fed herself."

"There's more to love that way," Tacante declared, refusing to share the news that there was a child growing within Hehaka. They would learn soon enough.

The greenleaf moon of late spring brought a strange stirring in the wasicun forts. Few wagons now rolled along the stolen road, and for the first time soldiers began to leave the forts and ride south before others arrived to take their place. Finally a band of Sahiyelas brought word the wasicuns were leaving the fort on Big Horn River.

"Hau!" a party of Minikowojus cried. "These forts will make good fires!"

"It may be a trick," Mahpiya Luta warned. "We'll send watchers."

Now was a time for caution, Tacante thought. Since the day the hundred were slain, the wasicuns had shown themselves to be clever. Hadn't they fought well from behind the wagon boxes? And Wamanon had paid the price for thinking the soldiers wouldn't guard their ponies.

As summer passed, though, the wasicuns marched out of each fort in turn. The words of the treaty were good, after all, many said. Tacante was among the warriors who rode down to look at the middle fort after the last bluecoats left it. The high log walls were deserted, and only scraps of corn and flour remained in the warehouses. They were ghost forts now, for the strange forest of crosses remained to mark the burials of the dead.

Strange that the wasicuns place their dead in the cold ground, Tacante thought. How can their spirits soar into the heavens and cross over to the other side?

"Maybe they're not there at all," Waawanyanka said. "We could dig and find out."

"Leave them," Tacante said, sensing a strangeness to the air. "Maybe their ghosts have not been given up. This is a good time for the Lakotas. We need no bad medicine."

So it was that the graveyard was left, but every other trace of the fort was erased by ax and flame. Mahpiya Luta stood on the watching hill as smoke climbed skyward. The Oglalas howled with pleasure as the walls collapsed in flaming heaps.

"It's a good day to be alive!" Sunka Sapa called, and Tacante echoed the shout. Others took it up until the hills resounded with the cry.

Most of the Sahiyelas broke their camps and moved toward Fort Laramie then. Talk of presents drew many of the others, as well. Mahpiya Luta and many of the Oglalas remained in the Big Horn country until the third fort was burned and the soldiers had returned to Platte River.

"Now we can touch the pen to the white man's paper," Mahpiya Luta declared. "Now I can believe he will leave us to live as we have before, on our own land in our own way."

The wasicuns at Fort Laramie welcomed Mahpiya Luta and the last of the Oglalas warmly. Many word writers gathered around to speak to the Cloud, and plenty of presents were distributed. Tacante translated the wasicun talk for many of the chiefs, but he longed to escape and see Hinkpila, his brother-friend. Soon enough Louis appeared, though he was surprised to find Tacante.

"I came to read the treaty to Red Cloud," Louis explained. "Ah, I'm glad to see you, brother. Your family is nearby. And I have news."

"First the treaty," Tacante said, noticing the impatient chiefs. "Then we'll share our news."

Louis then undertook the laborious task of explaining the meaning of the wasicun text to men who relied more on what was in a man's heart. Red Cloud didn't understand the need for another treaty, for, after all, the old one had promised the Lakotas that they would keep the land. This new paper said strange things. The Lakotas might keep the buffalo range north of Platte River and south in Kansas so long as the buffalo grazed there. So long as the buffalo remained? Who would outlive Tatanka?

There was talk of reservations, too. Already Sinte Gleska, the Spotted Tail, had picked out a good place to make his winter camps. The wasicuns promised a giveaway every summer at that place. Now Mahpiya Luta might have one as well.

Not everyone liked the treaty paper. Sunkawakan Witkotkoke argued against making camp at these agencies.

"The wasicuns will feed us like a pet horse," the strange Oglala complained. "Who rides with me to Tongue River? Which Lakota will be free?"

Many chose to go, but most stayed and accepted presents. There were good blankets to stave off winter chills, and many fine beads, looking glasses, kettles, and tools. Powder and shot for hunting was provided, and many new guns could be obtained in trade for buffalo hides.

Tacante paid little heed to it all. Louis had much news, and there were Hinhan Hota and little Itunkala to see, not to mention a mother and sister to visit, even if he would be restrained from speaking openly to either. As it turned out, Wicatankala was not with their mother.

"Has she gone to the women's lodge?" Tacante asked Hinhan Hota.

"She's gone to Hinkpila's lodge," the Owl explained. "She's his wife."

"Hau!" Tacante shouted, turning toward his grinning companion. "You've told me much, but you left out the best."

"I only wish you would have been here for the wedding feast, Brother," Louis answered. "Many were, though. I fear my father's poorer, and he laments that he's got so many sons yet to marry off."

"Ah, I have news, too," Tacante announced. "Hehaka carries our child. Winter will bring another Oglala to walk the earth."

Now it was Louis's turn to howl with delight. Hinhan Hota clasped his son's hands and shouted even louder. Even Itunkala seemed pleased. Until now the Mouse had remained quietly beside his father. Now the boy jumped onto Tacante's back and pounded the Heart unmercifully.

"It will be a son," Itunkala declared. "Perhaps he'll be bigger, though, than you and I. He should have a brave heart name, Ciye."

Tacante warmed at the sound of that word. Too long he had been among Hehaka's sisters. "Brother" sounded so very good. He grinned as he pried Itunkala loose. Then he set off to help make camp.

Tacante erected his lodge beside that of his father-in-law in the large circle that merged Wanbli Cannunpa's Oglalas with Hinhan Hota's Sicangus. Even as the Lakotas erected smoking racks for meat or stretched buffalo hides on willow frames, Mahpiya Luta led many of the people eastward toward his new agency at Camp Robinson. Sahiyelas journeyed south to Republican River, and the Dakotas went north into Paha Sapa.

"We should go, too," Hinhan Hota said. "Too long we've left the sacred circle of the stars. Winter should find us on White River, where there is good grass for the horses."

"Yes, Ate," Tacante said. "You should go. It is too long a journey for Hehaka. We'll stay here until the child is born."

"Too many bluecoats," Hinhan Hota warned. "We fought these men. They will remember."

"Hinkpila is here," Tacante argued. "He'll see we're not harmed."

"He is only part wasicun," the Owl pointed out. "Better you come with your people."

"White River is a hard place to be born, and winter is a starving time, Ate. I wish my son to live. I'll stay."

"Then you won't be alone," Hinhan Hota promised. "I, too, will stay."

As it turned out, most of the big camp stayed. With the war over, the young men rode out in desperate search for buffalo. There was little meat put by for winter, and much was needed, especially in the lodge of Wanbli Cannunpa. For Hehaka was not the only daughter married that winter.

It was little surprise to Tacante when Sunka Sapa lost his heart to pretty little Pehan, the Crane. Waawanyanka, though, had seldom even played his flute by the water walk, and he had come but once to invite Wakinyela, the Dove, to share his blanket. The Watcher was always the quiet one, though, and he brought two fine horses to Eagle Pipe and spoke his affection for Hehaka's older sister.

Last to be wedded was Hokala Huste. The Badger had grown serious now that he was a lance bearer, and often he'd spoken of how a man with such a short life ahead of him should never take a wife.

"I have no brother to look after my sons," Hokala said sadly.

"You have brothers," Tacante argued. "Haven't we spoken the words? You are kola."

"It's a hard thing to take a second woman into your lodge, and maybe little ones, too."

"Wouldn't Hehaka take her sister's child to her heart?" Tacante asked. "Go ask Wanbli Cannunpa to wed Sunlata."

"You knew?" Badger cried.

"She watches you whenever you pass," Tacante said, laughing. "As you watch her. Besides, the Pipe has no more daughters."

"It could have been someone else," Hokala said, glancing at the other lodges.

"Who? Only Iesni, the Silent One, is old enough, and she barely. Blue Creek emptied many Sicangu lodges."

"Yes," Hokala admitted. "So now we four will truly be brothers. Hau! And you soon will be a father, Tacante."

"You, too, in time, brother."

"Hau!" Hokala shouted. "It's enough to fill my heart with song!"

And so the three young Sicangus shared a wedding feast. Fewer presents were given away, for Wanbli Cannunpa had little to spare. The new lodges were sewn slowly, and only then because Tatanka answered Tacante's prayers and led him to a large herd of grazing buffalo. In the end, the tipis were finished before the snows grew too deep, and as winter settled in on Fort Laramie, nights were often greeted with the shy laughter of the newlyweds or the knowing whispers of their elders.

"Who would have thought it possible?" Tacante asked Louis as they stood together on the narrow porch of the trading post. "Not so long ago I thought surely I'd greet winter fighting bluecoats on some death-covered hill. Now I wait to bring a son into the world. Surely Wakan Tanka is a mystery."

"Truly," Louis agreed. "I never question things, though."

"No?"

"It's best. This is a good time, and I'm thankful. If tomorrow bad news arrives, well, I'll worry about it then. Just now I have a pretty wife to keep me happy, a family close by, and the best man I've every known to take me hunting."

"Ah, soon the snows will be too deep," Tacante muttered.

"Snows melt, Tacante. Summer will come."

"Yes, Hinkpila, it will."

Chapter Fifteen

As Hehaka's belly swelled with the growing child, Tacante felt strangely different. Always before, his eyes had looked to the buffalo hunt and the warrior trail. Now more and more he recalled the words of old He Hopa. He pounded the curing herbs to quiet a sick child's cough, and he drove fevers from the brows of Hinkpila's spectacled brother Philip.

For most, that time after the warring was good. For once there was enough to eat. The wounds of the young men healed, and even in the north, where the Crows now resumed their horse raids, few lodges filled with the mourning cries of the women.

It was not so everywhere, though. Louis brought word of the bluecoat battles in Kansas and the treaty lands beyond. It was there that the long-haired soldier chief Custer had struck the winter camp of old Black Kettle's Sahiyelas. The chief and his wife were dead. Many others, too. The soldiers had taken many captives to their forts, so the suffering was certain to continue.

"Ayyy! It's Blue Creek again" Hokala cried when Tacante shared the news. "These were the people attacked at Sand Creek. Wakan Tanka makes their road hard."

"And short," Tacante added. "The Sahiyelas touched the pen so that their people might live. Ayyy! The wasicun words mean nothing."

But while the soldiers now battled hostile bands of Sahiyelas on the Platte, in Kansas, and in northern Colorado Territory, the Lakotas remained at peace. The wasicun chiefs wished no more fights with Mahpiya Luta!

Tacante turned his attentions to the approaching birth. Many times he walked alone in the cold, snow-covered hills, searching for a dreaming. He smoked the pipe and made prayers that Wakan Tanka might send a strong son to the lodge of Buffalo Heart. Finally, when Hehaka went to the women's lodge, Tacante rode high into the hills and began his starving. Even as he cut his flesh and pleaded for a dream, he searched the wind for some trace of a child's first cry.

The dream was a long time coming. Tacante sat beside a small fire and shivered as the wind slashed at his face with its icy claws. Even breathing was difficult, and his feet and legs grew numb. Then, at last, he closed his eyes, and Tatanka spoke to his spirit.

"Hear me, Heart of the People," the vision beast said as it thundered across the plains. "Once I was many. Now my sons are struck down in great numbers. Tonska, I and you will live only so long as we are strong."

Tacante felt a great sadness as the vision filled with slaughtered animals.

"Yours must be a son to learn the old ways," Tatanka called. "Teach him to hold the ash bow and to smoke the pipe, offering tobacco in the sacred way. Give him tall horses to ride, for his road will be a hard one."

I know, Tatanka, Tacante silently answered. *And I will do as you say.*

Tacante was then roused from his trance by the strong arms of Hokala. The Badger helped the Heart rise.

"Brother, you have a son," Hokala announced. "Strong like his father, Wanbli Cannunpa says."

Tacante grinned, then followed Badger to where their horses waited. Together they rode back to the fort.

Already a crowd had collected outside the women's lodge. Tacante greeted friends and relatives and spoke with Hokala before joining Louis.

"So now you're a father, Brother," Louis said, gripping Tacante's hands. "Maybe I'll one day have a child. Then we'll take them hunting and speak of the old days when we, too, were small."

"Yes," Tacante agreed. "That will be a fine time."

Pehan, the Crane, then beckoned Tacante. She held in her arms a bundle of cloth that covered the Heart's tiny son. He held the infant but a moment. It was long enough to know the greatest sensation of pride felt in his young life.

"I would ask that you call him Tahca Wanbli," Eagle Pipe said as he motioned for Pehan to return the baby to the safety of the warm tipi. "That was my father's name."

Eagle Deer? His would be the quick feet of the deer and the far-seeing eyes of the eagle.

"A good name," Tacante agreed. "It honors my son."

"Now we must celebrate!" the chief declared. "I have given my grandson a name. Choose two of our best horses for the giveaway and find meat for the feast."

"Hau, Tunkasi," Tacante replied to his father-in-law. "It will be done."

Indeed, even as little Tahca Wanbli nestled at his mother's breast, the Oglala band of his grandfather celebrated with platters of fresh meat and the dancing and singing which properly followed the birth of a brave heart son.

"Never have I known such a happy time," Tacante told Hehaka when he held their son the first time. "Here is my heart come to life."

"And mine," Hehaka said, resting her head on Tacante's shoulder. "Surely we'll have a good life, Husband."

It certainly seemed so. Spring brought relief from the ice and snow, and Wanbli Cannunpa announced it was time to strike out for the buffalo valleys.

"Tatanka, our uncle, will give his brothers to our rifles," Eagle Pipe declared. "Tacante will make the strong prayers, and the scouts will seek the buffalo."

The young men howled their approval, for all knew Tacante spoke with Tatanka in his dreams, and Bull Buffalo was sure to guide his Lakota brother to where the hunting was best.

Tacante struck his lodge and prepared to leave the hillside overlooking Fort Laramie and the North Platte. He now was nearing the beginning of his twenty-first year. A man who had counted many coups, who had a wife and son, and who wore the horned bonnet of old He Hopa carried the obligations of leadership. Even so, he found it hard to bid farewell to his brother, Hinkpila, to his only sister, and to the place where peace had been brought to the people after so many had died.

"My road is before me," Tacante explained when Louis suggested there was much a Lakota might do near the fort.

"And mine is here," Louis explained, pointing to the shelves of goods in the trading post. "Take this to help remember me," Louis added, presenting a fine new Winchester rifle and two boxes of shells. "I'd hoped to give it to you when we rode together into the hills to hunt elk. Buffalo will be a truer test for a gun, though."

"Hau, Hinkpila," Tacante responded. "I'll bring you the first hide."

Tacante now began the great cycle of Lakota life. Following the winter rest, the people set out after the buffalo. This spring, hunting renewed the stocks of food and provided hides for new lodges and clothes. The young men sometimes gathered wild ponies to enrich their herds. Sometimes, too, the Crows came down, and there was a lively bit of horse raiding or even a good fight.

Tacante bore great responsibilities during the buffalo hunt, for it was his duty to oversee the pipe ceremonies and make the prayers to Tatanka. He Hopa had always urged the hunters to undergo Inipi, the rite of rebirth, whenever the people began any great task, and Tacante deemed it important before the vital life-giving buffalo hunt.

"Many of us have forgotten to follow the sacred path of our grandfathers," he told the men. "We have fought and killed in anger. We've taken up the iron guns and lead bullets of our enemies. Wakan Tanka must think that we have forgotten that all we are comes from the Great Mystery."

"No," Hokala insisted.

"It's not true," others argued.

"Then it's time we cleanse ourselves," Tacante declared.

Inipi was a ritual of purification, of ridding the body and the soul of all that offended the spirits. It was an old rite, and Tacante himself had undergone it often. Even the wasicun doctors at Fort Laramie praised the great curing powers of the sweat lodge, even if they failed to understand the many prayers or the importance of doing all that was required.

Tacante himself oversaw the construction of the lodge. To begin with, a round framework was built of twelve to sixteen young willows. The trees reminded the Lakotas that leaves might die in the winter, but they were reborn in spring, even as a man might be reborn through casting off his old self. The willows were staked into the ground in a circle, then bent over to make an inverted bowl. They formed quadrants, one each for the four directions—north, south, east, and west—and the four divisions of the universe—the two-legged, four-legged, and winged creatures, plus all the things of the earth. An opening was made in the east, for the light of all knowledge came from that direction.

Ten paces from the entrance of the sweat lodge, Tacante built a sacred fireplace. He laid four sticks running east and west, then added four more running north and south. Next he built a tipi of sticks over them and kindled a flame. Afterward he put rocks out to mark each of the directions, and stacked other rocks on top.

Tacante dug a hole in the center of the sweat lodge. He then used the dirt to form a sacred path leading east. At the end of this path, he formed an earth mound. Meanwhile others covered the willow framework with buffalo hides, leaving a single hide over the entrance like a door.

As each pole or rock or stick was placed, sacred prayers were made to Wakan Tanka. But it was only when those undergoing Inipi arrived that the ceremony began in earnest.

Like all the Lakota sacred ceremonies, Inipi began with the smoking of the pipe. Tacante entered the lodge alone with the pipe. He passed around to the west and sat down. He then placed pinches of tobacco in the four sides of the central hole, honoring the directions. A sacred coal was passed inside, and Tacante saw it placed in the center. He then placed sweet grass on the coal, allowing the sacred smoke to rise so that he could rub it over his body and the pipe. Everything was now wakan, and any bad medicine in the lodge was driven out.

Tacante invoked the help of the winged creatures of the west, for it was they who brought the purifying waters. Afterward he offered tobacco to the four directions, to the heavens, and to Mother Earth. Outside, the others howled their approval, knowing it was the pipe ceremony that brought power into the sweat lodge.

Satisfied, Tacante returned outside, following the sacred path until he reached the mound. He then placed the pipe on the mound and instructed those wishing purification to enter the lodge.

The first men came forward singly. Each wore only a modest breechclout, for ornaments of the past didn't belong. Hair was left loose and unbraided. One by one they entered, bowed low in the doorway, and recited the prayer of the humble. It was right that a man understand he was nothing compared to Wakan Tanka, the Great Mystery.

Inside, the men moved sun-wise around the central altar and sat on the floor. Sage had been strewn around, giving a pleasant odor to the place. Tacante followed last, taking his place on the east beside the door. For a time they remained silent, thinking of the goodness that surrounded them and the great power of Wakan Tanka, the maker of all things. Then Hehaka, as was proper for a medicine woman, handed in the pipe, and Hokala, who was seated on the western side, placed it in front of him.

Now Hehaka used a forked stick to bring in the heated rocks. As each in turn was laid upon the altar, Hokala touched the pipe to the rock, and the men made thanks. The first rock symbolized Wakan Tanka, and each of the others represented heaven or Mother Earth or a direction. Finally all the rocks were stacked in the center, and all things in the universe were thanked for making up the Lakotas' world.

Hokala then took up the pipe and spoke the sacred prayers to Wakan Tanka, heaven, Mother Earth, and the four directions. He then puffed, allowing the smoke to cover his body before passing the pipe along to the next person in line. Often father and son, brothers and cousins would undergo Inipi together, for it was a shared spiritual rebirth, and many felt bonded to those around them. After the pipe was passed around the circle, Hokala purified it again with the seven prayers and emptied the ashes at the edge of the circle. Badger then passed the pipe sun-wise to Tacante, who turned it to the east and passed it to Hehaka outside the door.

Hehaka refilled the pipe and placed it on the sacred mound with the stem pointing west, symbolically invoking the powers of that direction. She then closed the hide door, leaving the lodge in total darkness.

Now Hokala, being on the west side, began the prayers for help. Wakan Tanka's help was sought first. Then all the other spirits and elements of the world, even down to the rocks and the trees, were respectfully thanked for their many good deeds and great help.

Tacante then sprinkled water on the glowing rocks, once for Wakan Tanka, again for the heavens, a third time for Mother Earth, and a fourth for the sacred pipe. Steam began to fill the lodge. Tacante added sprigs of sage and handfuls of sweet grass so that a pleasant odor passed among them.

It didn't take long for the small lodge to grow very hot. Sweat beaded on chests and brows, driving out all the misdeeds and bad thoughts. Tacante felt oddly light-headed, and he saw the new life coming to the shadowy faces of his companions.

Now Hehaka opened the door of the lodge, allowing blinding light to flood the interior. In this way, Tacante was reminded of the knowledge given man in the first of the four great ages. Helpers brought water, and Tacante took a small drink, then splashed some over his forehead and chest before passing it along to the next man. Each did much the same. Then the pipe was brought back, and Hokala took it up and made the purifying prayers once more.

Four times the pipe was passed, and four times prayers were made. After the pipe was returned to the sacred mound, Tacante added water to the rocks, and the steam drove out the bad thoughts from the people.

During Inipi, Tacante was careful to remind his companions of the sacred power of the fire, the purifying powers of the smoke, the great energy of Thunderbird, and the reverence Lakotas have for all things. He then began the final prayers of thanks, knowing that through this understanding of all the elements of life, a man might return to the sacred path and be reborn as a purified soul.

For three days the Lakotas underwent Inipi. Tacante smiled as he observed small children peering under the buffalo hides in search of the great mystery of rebirth. When they were older, they, too, would enter the sweat lodge. No effort was made to drive them away from that sacred place, for there was nothing they might hear which they shouldn't know. To see fathers or older brothers suffering and yet shouting thanks was puzzling, but a child was never too young to begin wondering about the mysteries of the sacred path.

Perhaps it was Inipi that brought success to the Oglala hunters that spring. Or maybe in the wasicun-fighting days, the buffalo had grown less suspicious of the sight of Lakota hunters. Tacante dreamed often of

Tatanka, and he told the people Bull Buffalo wished his nephews to grow strong and tall to face the hard times ahead.

"Hard times?" many asked. "They are over."

So it seemed for a time. Wanbli Cannunpa's band grew as the power of Tacante's medicine drew other small bands of Oglala and Sicangu hunters. Under the waning chokecherry moon of summer, a great gathering of the Lakotas took place in Paha Sapa, the Black Hills. There, at Bear Lodge, a great flat-topped mountain with high, steep sides, the sun dance was held.

Many people danced around the sacred circle, but only a few were called to undertake the sun dance itself. It involved great pain and much suffering, and it wasn't for the young or the weak to try. It was also a renewing rite, but while some danced to bring good things to the people, others danced to drive sickness from a friend or relative. It was a great thing to participate in the sun dance, and many of the young men offered themselves this time. Tacante and Hokala were among them.

Wanbli Cannunpa himself led them to the sacred cottonwood. Each sun dancer was instructed in the sacred medicine rites before undergoing Inipi. Next he made many prayers. Finally his friends and relatives offered presents and painted his body. Dancers usually blackened their arms, for here was the bad heart to be driven out. Faces and trunks were stained red. Small slits were then made in the flesh of the chest, through which small flat pegs were run. Each end of the peg was attached to one end of a buffalo-hide thong. The two thongs joined to form a strip that was attached to the sacred cottonwood in the center of the dance circle.

Tacante endured all this without complaint, for the Heart of the People should be willing to undergo suffering. Now, as he stood beside Hokala, watching blood from his chest trickle down across his belly, he was called upon to follow the other dancers in this sacred undertaking. The first dancers bore heavy burdens or buffalo skulls or heavy rocks. They whirled about madly, screaming their pain through eagle-bone whistles so that the eerie noise flooded the scene.

When Tacante was called to dance, he did so readily. At the end of the dance, though, he stretched back so that the thongs pulled at the pegs and opened the flesh of his chest. So long as a man could, he danced in this manner, giving up his blood and enduring the pain so that the people might be purified. Only when a man grew weak was he to stretch the thongs to where flesh could no longer resist the force placed on the pegs. Then the dancer painfully ripped himself loose.

The first dancers blew their shrill whistles and danced through the morning. Then the first broke himself loose. Another followed, and three more freed themselves a bit later. Tacante screamed his pain through the whistle and went on, determine to endure. Hokala broke himself loose around midday and collapsed in a heap. Two other dancers tried, but only managed to collapse. Relatives arrived and helped break the bonds.

Tacante continued. As blood deepened the red color of his chest and dripped across the ground, he grew light-headed. He saw many strange beasts galloping along. Finally he beheld Tatanka.

"Brave up, Tacante," Bull Buffalo urged. "See what danger awaits us."

A vision of a smoking mountain appeared, thundering along the banks of Yellowstone River. Great flashes of lightning reached out of the mountain to strike down elk, deer, buffalo, and finally even Tatanka.

The vision faded, and Tacante felt his legs grow numb. He blinked his eyes and tried to see his companions. There were none. He was alone.

"Ayyy!" he screamed through the whistle as he suddenly flung himself back. The left-hand peg broke through his skin, but the right-hand peg remained. Pain tore at Tacante's chest, and he swallowed hard. He screamed again, then used his final ounce of strength to stretch the thong. The skin ripped apart, and Tacante fell backward against the ground. He stared up at a pair of painted faces and grinned. Then he lost consciousness.

Four summers came and went, and Tacante thought little of the thunder mountain roaring along the Yellowstone. He'd been too feverish, after all. If He Hopa had been there to question the dream, perhaps its warning might have been seen.

As it was, Tacante found himself an honored warrior and medicine man. His dreams led the hunters to game and warned of winter blizzards. He spent spring and summer on the plain, hunting and living the old free way. In autumn he visited his family, who were camped with Sinte Gleska at the agency the wasicuns had set up for the Sicangus.

Afterward Tacante wintered on Platte River near Fort Laramie or headed into the Big Horns.

Those years brought much personal happiness. Twice more Hehaka's belly swelled, and two more sons came to walk the earth beside Tacante. Cetan Kinyan, Flying Hawk, came first. His was a name well given, for that boy was upon a horse before he could walk, and his keen eyes noted everything. Hinhancika, the younger boy, was Itunkala reborn. The Little Owl was forever in mischief, vexing father and mother, but old Wanbli Cannunpa took over the child's raising, and the Owl soon learned to temper his exploring with a bit of caution.

The first word of wasicuns on Yellowstone River arrived that spring. A young Hunkpapa brought news that peace speakers had come asking that mapmakers be allowed to ride along the river. It soon became clear that they weren't there to make a map, though. Wagons full of men set poles in the ground and marked the way for a road.

"It's like Platte River," Waawanyanka then announced. "Such men came after the Powder River fighting. Soon the iron horse followed."

"Hau!" Tacante shouted. The dream came back to him. The wasicuns were bringing another iron horse road into the Lakota country.

"No!" Wanbli Cannunpa cried when Tacante explained. "This won't be. We'll keep the mapmakers out."

It wasn't so easy, though. When the peace speakers couldn't persuade the Lakotas to let the mapmakers peacefully cross the country, soldiers were sent along. Many soldiers. And leading them was the very same bluecoat chief Custer, called Long Hair, who had killed old Black Kettle on treaty land down south.

"Hau, we'll show this Long Hair how Lakotas fight!" Hokala cried.

"Hau!" the young men shouted. "It's a good day to die."

Tacante assembled forty warriors, but they soon saw that the soldiers had learned many lessons since the hundred were slain. All the bluecoats carried the new lay-down-and-load guns, and whenever the mapmakers made camp, a thunder gun was sure to be nearby. Scouts combed the countryside for ambushes, and there were fifteen hundred soldiers and many wagon people.

Tacante's band seldom got within shooting range of the bluecoats. Once or twice they pulled up stakes or ran off some horses, but they had little luck against the soldiers. Brave young men appeared as decoys, but the bluecoats didn't follow. A few soldiers were killed by the Hunkpapas, and Sunkawakan Witkotkoke trapped some once. But Long Hair didn't come out and fight. The mapmakers finished their map and went home.

Tacante's heart filled with despair, for already the Sahiyelas complained that the iron horse was chasing all the game from Platte River. Then Tatanka appeared in the Heart's dreams. Bull Buffalo stood atop the thunder mountain, pounding it flat with his mighty hoofs.

"Things've gone sour for the railroad," Louis explained when Tacante erected his winter lodge near Fort Laramie. "Seems the iron horse is stopping in the Dakotas."

Tacante might have warmed with that news, but he couldn't. The Dakotas, the wasicuns called that land. The name attested to the fact that it belonged to the Lakotas' cousins. The iron horse had stopped, but for how long? Those who had seen Long Hair said he was a man with hungry eyes. Hungry for a fight. And who was there to fight but the Lakota people?

Chapter Sixteen

Long Hair Custer wasn't long idle. He and his bluecoat horse soldiers were on the march again that next summer. This time they struck deep into the heart of Lakota country, into Paha Sapa itself. Here was a place forbidden to wasicuns by both the Fort Laramie treaties, but this wasicun chief cared nothing for the sacred word of the treaty makers. Just as the eagle chief Harney had killed the innocents at Blue Creek, this Custer now violated the Black Hills.

Only a few scattered Lakotas saw the soldiers. Hunters seeking game or boys on vision quests stood scant chance of stopping a bluecoat army. All the Lakotas could do was stare angrily as these thieves came into the sacred country, shooting down the animals and felling the trees. Some dug in the ground or scratched at the streambeds, searching for the yellow powder which turned wasicuns into crazy men. In time the bluecoats turned from the sacred lands.

"Hau!" the Lakotas cried. "Wakan Tanka has driven the wasicuns from our home."

The soldiers had wounded the people deeply, though. Soon enough the true danger came.

Tacante was visiting Hinhan Hota's band at Spotted Tail when word came of wasicun miners stealing yellow rocks in Paha Sapa.

"Surely this can't be!" Tacante exclaimed. "Tell your soldier friends to drive the thieves out, Ate!"

Hinhan Hota frowned gravely.

"We have fought our war, Tacante," the Owl said wearily. "We've suffered and we've died. Haven't you seen the power of the wasicuns? They come along the Platte like summer locusts. You can kill a thousand, and a thousand more will follow. It's for them to do, for them to say, my son. Ask Sinte Gleska of the power he's seen in the great wasicun villages. Ask Mahpiya Luta if he has heart to fight again."

"Paha Sapa is our heart," Tacante argued. "Ate, where will we hunt? Where will our children be born? Here, where there are no trees, where there is only dry grass to eat?"

"It's for the young men to fight," Hinhan Hota muttered soberly. "But think hard, my son. You have a wife and little ones to care for. Remember Blue Creek."

"I remember," Tacante said angrily. "It's because of that I could never live off the wasicuns' presents, turning away from the sacred way."

"It's a hard road you set your feet upon."

"Ah, what's hard, Ate? I can't cut myself off from Wakan Tanka. I am a Tokala, aren't I? It's the difficult thing I am supposed to do."

"Living here will be difficult, too," the Owl declared. "Knowing my son won't come to share the autumn moons in my lodge will be hard. As is growing used to the taste of cow meat."

Tacante bowed his head. He understood. Hinhan Hota also faced a difficult trail. Perhaps, after all, it was easier to fight. Tacante spent little time wondering, for he knew there was but one direction he could take.

He gathered the little ones that afternoon and spoke of making a winter camp in Paha Sapa.

"Ate, we won't go to Hinkpila's fort?" Tahca Wanbli asked. The boy had not yet celebrated his sixth winter on the earth, but he recalled the fine times spent with his aunt and uncle on Platte River.

"No, little one," Tacante said gravely. "We must drive the thieves from our sacred places."

"I, too, will fight," the child vowed, drawing the small knife Itunkala had given him.

"Not this time," Tacante said, hoisting his eldest onto one shoulder and placing a hand on the heads of the two younger boys. "You're small yet. The time may come."

Indeed, Tacante feared it would.

He was dismantling the lodge when Itunkala appeared. The boy was fourteen now, but still short and frightfully thin. His small size was deceptive, though, for there was iron in his grip, and he rode like a whirlwind.

"Brother, you aren't leaving?" the Mouse called.

"Yes," Tacante confessed. "There's much that needs doing."

"You go to fight the wasicun thieves, then?"

"Yes. To guard Paha Sapa for the people."

"The soldiers go to chase the thieves from the sacred land," Itunkala explained. "They take many of the young men of the agency with them to scout. I thought to join them."

"Ah, and who was it who first scratched the streams, who spoke of the yellow powder? Long Hair Custer. Everyone knows now how he rode into Paha Sapa, how he hungers to steal our country."

"I won't scout for them," Mouse vowed.

"It's good, little brother. I wouldn't like to think you put on the blue coat and rode with our enemies."

"Are the wasicuns our enemies again? I've made friends among the trader's sons. There is our brother, Hinkpila, too."

"His heart is turned toward us by his grandmother's blood."

"There are good men among the soldiers."

"Ah, I've seen many brave bluecoats, Itunkala. One I killed. But their chiefs have bad hearts and hungry eyes. We'll fight them again soon."

"Then it's for me to come with you," Itunkala said solemnly. "I've ridden to the buffalo hunt with you, Tacante. I can shoot the bow, and I know hard living."

"You're young."

"Yes, and small," Itunkala admitted, staring at his twiglike legs. "But you said you, too, were small, and I will grow."

"Then go and speak of it to our father," Tacante advised as he stripped the buffalo-hide covering from the lodge. "Know that you're welcome to come, but I find no dishonor in a man who chooses to stay."

"Yes," the Mouse said, knowing Tacante spoke of Hinhan Hota.

By the time Tacante had arranged the poles into a pony drag for the children and collected his horses, Itunkala had returned.

"Ate says I leave his heart cold and empty," the Mouse said. "I'm old enough to choose my path. I go with my brother."

Tacante gazed back at the gap in the camp circle left by his dismantled lodge. Tasiyagnunpa stood there, gazing sorrowfully at her departing sons. And grandsons. For a moment Tacante thought to leave Hehaka and the boys in his mother's care, but who would strike his lodge to follow a warrior who left his own children behind? And what safety was an agency camp? Black Kettle was on treaty land, after all.

Tacante wasn't the only Lakota who journeyed to Paha Sapa that autumn. As he erected his lodge in an ancient camp on the southern edge of the hills, he saw a band of black-faced warriors in the streambed below.

"Hau, Lakotas!" Tacante cried.

"Hau!" a light-skinned warrior answered. Even now there was a red-tailed hawk tied in his hair.

"Sunkawakan Witkotkoke, you, too, have come to fight the wasicuns," Tacante called as he hurried down the hillside.

"Hau, it's Tacante!" Waawanyanka howled. Hokala and Sunka Sapa were there as well, together with twenty young Oglalas.

"Now we'll punish these thieves!" the Horse promised as he greeted Tacante warmly. "Already we've killed three. Come, bring your lodge to the camp."

"Yes," Hokala urged. "Sunlata grows anxious to show you our son."

Tacante howled loudly, for a birthing was always a good omen for any undertaking. Hokala and Sunka Sapa helped break down the lodge, and soon Tacante was following Sunkawakan Witkotkoke again. The little ones rode along behind one of their uncles, and Hehaka slapped her buckskin mare into a fast trot. Soon she'd be among her sisters.

One surprise remained for Tacante. He expected a small circle of lodges. Instead Wanbli Cannunpa's entire band was there, together with many young Oglalas and Sicangus from Red Cloud and Spotted Tail agencies. Boys of fifteen and sixteen could scarcely remember the desperate fighting at Powder River. Their hearts were full of warrior songs, and they were eager to follow Hokala, the Tokala lance bearer, of Sunkawakan Witkotkoke, the Oglala strange one. Now that Tacante was there, too, they sang brave heart songs. Strong medicine would ride at their side.

Tacante's heart warmed to know Hehaka was among her family once more. Eagle Pipe would not ride to battle, but he knew how to keep a camp in order, and the little ones would be safe under the watchful eye of their grandfather.

That was a comfort, for the soldiers soon tired of chasing the miners from Paha Sapa. It was foolish to try, one bluecoat told Tacante. Once among the wasicun villages, the thieves were set free.

"We'll punish them," Tacante swore.

It was a grim business, and dangerous, too. The wasicun miners carried rapid-firing Winchesters like the one Hinkpila had given Tacante. Many were good shots, and often a reckless young man charged a wasicun camp and was shot dead. Sunkawakan Witkotkoke drove bands of wasicuns from the hills as he might have driven hares from a thicket.

Tacante preferred caution. These thieves didn't deserve the brave heart fight. No, it was best to catch the miners off alone or perhaps eating their food.

Tacante and Hokala took several young men with them one morning. Waawanyanka, always the keen-eyed one, had spotted miners digging along a nearby stream. The Heart watched carefully as two hairy-faced wasicuns kept guard with rifles as several barebacked companions scooped sand out of the stream with flat tin pans.

It's a bad day for you, wasicuns, Tacante thought as he stared at his black-faced companions. Hokala silently pointed to the right-hand guard, and Tacante chose the one on the left. He then signaled Itunkala and the other young men to wait.

Tacante and Hokala dismounted and wove their way through the tall pines toward the stream. They were still many paces away when an old man suddenly shouted and tossed his pan in the air. He held a large yellow rock in his hand. The guards rushed down to the stream to join the crazed wasicuns.

"Ayyy!" Hokala cried, jumping atop his man and killing him with a single knife thrust.

"Ayyy!" Tacante answered, raising his rifle and shooting the other guard through the back of the head.

Now the young men screamed and charged the stunned miners.

The older wasicuns immediately splashed across the stream in a frantic effort to lose themselves among the thick trees beyond. One escaped. Two others were cut down by arrows. A younger wasicun threw Sunkmanitu Tanka, the Wolf, from his horse and fought to capture the fleeing animal. Tacante gave a howl and fired his rifle again. The wasicun fell sideways, clutching his side. Wolf fell on the man and put an end to him.

Of the miners, only a few boys remained. Three were scarcely as old as Itunkala, and two others had yet to grow whiskers on their chins. All five fell to their knees and pleaded for mercy.

"Was Uncle Ben made us come," a youngster sobbed. "We knew this was Injun country, but they said we could get rich. Lord help us!"

The boys were frozen in terror by the sight of the Lakotas scalping their companions.

"Tacante, what do we do with them?" Itunkala asked.

The other young men were equally confused.

"They're young," Tacante said. "Perhaps they'll learn."

"My brother, who died at Blue Creek, never had a chance to learn," Hokala argued. "Wasicuns only learn when they are dead."

Tacante looked deeply into his bad-hearted friend's eyes. They both knew, handed Winchesters, these same boys might easily slay a Lakota. Still, it was a bright day, and Wakan Tanka had given a victory into Tacante's hands.

"We'll do as on the stolen road," the Heart declared. "Take their clothes, their shoes, all their belongings. Leave them to walk naked from this place."

The young men laughed at the thought, but Hokala objected.

"They will come back," Badger complained.

"Then they'll die," Tacante said. He then translated his decision, and the young wasicuns stared fearfully at the surrounding warriors.

"We'll freeze, if we don't starve first," a red-haired boy answered for his friends. "It's thirty, forty miles. Can't expect us to walk all that way naked."

"It's for you to choose," Tacante said, drawing his knife from its sheath. "We can end the pain."

The redheaded youngster stared hard at the sharp blade of the knife.

He then slid his suspenders off his shoulders and dropped his trousers. The others followed his example, and soon there were five naked wasicuns splashing along the stream, their pale, skinny bodies drawing laughs from men who moments before might have brought their death.

"I'll watch them," Hokala said as Tacante turned toward his horse. "I, too," Sunkmanitu Tanka added.

"Then you should take the wasicun rifles," Tacante declared, motioning for Itunkala to hand over the prized guns. "When we find their horses, you shall have the pick."

"Hau!" Wolf shouted.

"Next time I decide," Hokala said, grabbing the offered rifle and turning away.

Winter fell on Paha Sapa early that year, and the cold sent most of the thieves hurrying back to the towns springing up on the fringe of the hills. The snows were deep, and many of the Lakotas camped in Wanbli Cannunpa's village left for the agencies. Sunka Sapa and Waawanyanka both had small ones not used to hardship. They departed. Tacante remained, though it tore at his heart to see his children shivering in their elk and buffalo hides when the icy wind swept down from the north. Often the Heart huddled with one or the other of the boys, filling their ears with brave heart tales or stories of Coyote or Rabbit. Itunkala sometimes blew his flute or sang in his gentle, soft voice.

"It's not so cold," Cetan Kinyan whispered as he clung to his father's side.

No, Tacante told himself. No pain was great when shared.

Spring promised better days. As the snows melted and the cottonwoods and willows greened, game returned. Men set out in threes and fours to shoot deer and elk. Tacante often brought plump geese or fat squirrels for the kettle. Then one morning Itunkala brought grave news.

"Sunka Sapa will not ride with us to hunt the buffalo," the Mouse explained.

Tacante felt an icy dart stab his heart. Always the Black Dog had been at his side, whether hunting or fighting bluecoats. Itunkala's contorted face told of grave news.

"Where?" Tacante asked.

"On Goose Creek," Itunkala explained. "Sunkawakan Witkotkoke is there now."

Tacante mounted his horse and rode off at a gallop. It was a half day's riding to Goose Creek, but Tacante crossed the hills and streams in half that time. What he saw there blackened his heart. The remains of Sunka Sapa's lodge lay in ashes. The small charred skeleton of his daughter lay wrapped in a buffalo hide. The Dog lay beside the creek, his body stripped and many bullet wounds attesting to the fight put up. Pehan, whose grace had earned her the name Crane, had been dragged into the underbrush. Her head had been crushed with a rock, and the killers had cut a ring from her hand.

"I had only a buffalo hide," Sunkawakan Witkotkoke said, pointing to Sunka Sapa. "I would have covered him."

"It's for me to do," Tacante said, laying his coat over his bloody friend. "Did they leave a trail?"

"A good one," the Horse said, pointing to muddy tracks in the creek. "Your brother will gather a war party. For this, many will die."

Tacante drew his knife and began slashing willow limbs to make a scaffold. There were rocks nearby. Sunka Sapa always liked high places. So did the girl he'd named Wanahcazi, Yellow Flower. But as he worked, Tacante found himself slashing not willow bark but wasicun throats. He stumbled to the creek and stared at his wild-eyed face. It might have been Hokala demanding the deaths of the boy miners. Badger wouldn't be the only one to speak for killing now.

Tacante finished the scaffolds that afternoon. Hehaka and her sisters bathed the bodies and dressed them in the finest garments possessed by the band. Finally Wanbli Cannunpa spoke prayers, and Tacante danced, hoping whatever power he possessed might salve the tortured souls of his slaughtered relatives.

For three days the Lakotas mourned. On the fourth Sunkawakan Witkotkoke led a dozen warriors along the trail of the killers. The faces and hands of the Lakotas were blackened with ashes. It would be a bad heart raid, and much blood was certain to be shed.

The Horse was little changed. He sang warrior songs and urged the sharp-eyed boys to watch for sign. Tacante and Hokala rode on relentlessly. They'd seen in Pehan's silent face her sisters, and the burned child might have been their own.

The wasicuns might have escaped had rain come to Paha Sapa. Many times their trail grew faint, but the rocky ground told its tale, and the Lakotas at last came upon a party of wasicuns gathered around a cook fire.

"It's a good day to die," Hokala declared as he filled his new rifle's magazine.

"A bad day to be a wasicun," Itunkala added as he pointed out three children skipping flat rocks across a pond.

"We kill them all," Hokala growled, angrily turning to Tacante.

"Even them?" Itunkala asked, pointing to the children.

"Is Flower forgotten?" Hokala barked. "All!"

"All," Tacante echoed, hardening his resolve.

The Horse then screamed out a war cry and led the charge. The dozen Lakotas spilled out of the trees and fell upon the surprised miners like a cyclone. Rifles exploded, and lances struck hard. A woman screamed as Hokala fell upon her. Itunkala raced to cut off the fleeing children, two boys and a girl. They stumbled into the pond, then gazed up silently as Mouse notched an arrow.

"My face is black with death," Itunkala chanted, but he could not release the arrow. Tacante struggled to free himself from the grasp of a huge, red-bearded wasicun who was wearing the silver ring Sunka Sapa had given Pehan.

"Billy, run!" the red-beard shouted.

Tacante managed to turn his knife and cut into the big-bellied thief. The wasicun screamed in agony as the blade penetrated deeper, opening him up like a gutted deer. Tacante pulled back as the dying giant rolled away.

"Papa!" one of the boys shouted as he raced from the pond.

Tacante turned toward the frightened child, but three quick shots from a revolver downed the boy. The Heart didn't glance toward the shooter. He didn't want to know who had spared him the task.

Hokala took charge of the other two little ones. The Badger grimly covered their faces with his big hands and stopped their breathing.

"It was for me to do that," Itunkala said when Tacante reached the pond. "But they were so small."

"It's good you couldn't blacken your heart to them," Tacante declared. "Soon I fear we'll all have bad faces, and there will be no softness left."

As the brothers gazed back at their companions angrily slashing the corpses, they shared a muffled moan.

It wasn't possible, as Hinhan Hota had warned, to stem the flood of wasicuns pouring into Paha Sapa. More and more of them came. Mutilated bodies only made them quicker to fire at the first sign of a bronze-skinned rider.

Word came that the wasicuns were sending chiefs to Mahpiya Luta's agency to make peace. Sunkawakan Witkotkoke and Wanbli Cannunpa agreed such peace talk should be heard, and the camp was packed up.

Red Cloud spoke for most of the Lakotas when the peace commissioners offered to buy Paha Sapa.

"Why buy what you are already stealing?" he asked.

Others declared the land was already lost and suggested asking a high price.

But when the warriors gathered, angry voices rose.

"What of the treaty?" some cried.

"You steal our land again and again, kill the buffalo, and now you speak of peace when we fight back?"

Sinte Gleska, Spotted Tail, rode forward to urge calm. His was a voice to be heard, for he, too, had fought as a brave heart youth. Now he had seen too many things to dream of winning a war against the wasicuns.

"Ah, we can never sell the heart of the earth!" Hokala shouted.

"Hau!" the Oglala Little Big Man cried. "It's a good time to begin a war!"

Begin? Tacante asked himself. When did the fighting stop? He'd been born in a time of trial, and it had never ceased.

Blue-coated soldiers now lined up to protect the peace speakers, and it seemed more blood would stain the earth. But again Sinte Gleska spoke, and peace prevailed at Red Cloud Agency.

Chapter Seventeen

As was proper before all great undertakings, Tacante built a sweat lodge and underwent Inipi. As the heat burned away his sadness and restored him to the sacred way, he tried not to think of the stolen heart of the country, the hungry-eyed Long Hair, or the peace speakers who couldn't understand there were things which a man didn't sell.

Half a moon later Tacante rode slowly along Platte River toward where the sprawling buildings of Fort Laramie rose from the grassy plain. Itunkala was at his side, babbling a hundred thoughts at once. *Soon,* Tacante thought, *I must find another name for this brother who is growing to be a man.* His dark, bare shoulders were now broad and powerful, and if his voice still cracked and grunted, well, Tacante remembered his own had done the same.

A few paces behind, young Tahca Wanbli rode. A boy of seven snows should ride his own pony, and Tacante had cut out a fine pinto for his firstborn. Hehaka followed the pony drag that carried the younger boys. Hokala and his family came next. Then a few young agency men trailed their elders.

A party of soldiers rode alongside. These were recruits, and their young, worried faces betrayed the dread tales of Lakota butchery shared by the veterans.

"Them's Sioux!" a three-stripe had shouted.

Fear had instantly flashed across the young soldiers' faces. It was clear testimony to the bad heart tales kindled among the wasicuns. Even as the thieves stole Paha Sapa, they spoke of the murdering Indians who killed women and children. These same people shot Lakotas without thinking—killed people on their own land. The wasicuns truly dwelled in a crazed place. Their world had no circle, no heart.

The Lakotas were met at the approaches to the fort by a silver-bar chief who shouted angrily that here was a band of hostiles to be herded back to the reservation.

"Where's that fool interpreter, Jenkins?" the chief howled at a two-stripe. Hinkpila then appeared.

"Lieutenant?" Louis asked.

"Ask 'em why they've come!" the soldier chief shouted. "Tell 'em we've got to take their guns and get 'em along home."

"Talk to them yourself," Louis answered sharply. "This is Buffalo Heart, my Brule Sioux brother. I suspect he's come to hunt buffalo. The treaty gives him that right, Lieutenant. He's wintered here often, and he speaks good English. He's entitled, by the way, to wear a bonnet of thirty feathers to mark the coups he's counted. Most of 'em's been on white soldiers."

"We come peacefully," Tacante then announced. "I would share the buffalo hunt with Hinkpila, my brother. Here is Badger, Mouse, my wife, Deer Woman, and there are the others."

"We've heard of much killing in the Black Hills," the officer said, staring with cold eyes at his visitors. "You take up such nonsense here, I'll see you punished."

"You would punish me, wasicun?" Itunkala cried. "It's not me who's broken the treaty and stolen Paha Sapa."

Tacante silenced his brother, then turned to Louis.

"There will be no trouble from my people," Tacante said, folding his arms. "We are going to hunt soon. I would show my brother how the little ones are growing, and I would see my sister."

Louis insisted Tacante spoke straight.

"The whole bunch looks like they'd as soon slit my throat as chew a carrot," the soldier retorted.

"He'd kill you on the battlefield, sure enough," Louis agreed. "But not here. He's my guest, and you can be certain he is welcome."

The soldiers then went about their labors, and Tacante followed Hinkpila to the trading post his father had built. René Le Doux was gone now, headed to California with his wife and the younger children. Louis and Philip, the spectacled one, remained to operate the store.

After helping the Lakotas erect their lodges behind a horse corral, Louis led the way inside the small house he'd built behind the store. Tacante greeted Wicatankala, his sister, and held the small son and daughter called Tom and Grace.

"They grow strong," Tacante observed when little Grace gripped his finger tightly with her small hand.

"Ah, it's the children keep our hearts young, you know."

"I pray our sons will share the buffalo hunt as we have."

"Yes," Louis agreed as he led the way to a back room.

"But it's a bad time to come here now, eh?"

"The soldiers are angry," Louis explained. "There was almost a fight at Red Cloud's agency this spring, and reinforcements have been sent out to Fort Fetterman."

Tacante frowned. He knew, of course, of the bad feelings exchanged at Red Cloud. As for the new fort built where the stolen road met Platte River, Tacante had been told of how it was named for the boastful eagle chief killed on the hill of the hundred slain. Strange that the sodiers should make heroes out of foolish chiefs!

"Crazy Horse's in the Big Horn country, I hear," Louis said, trying to break the silence. "You've ridden with him often."

"I will again," Tacante answered.

"Be a hard fight this time, Misun."

Tacante stared at Hinkpila. When had even Mastincala been a little brother? There was a fond, almost fatherly glow in Louis's eyes, and Tacante let the word stand.

"I wish to be a man of peace," Tacante said, "but everywhere the wasicuns steal our land, slaughter Tatanka, our uncle. I starve myself for visions, but none come. There's nothing left but to seek the high country where Thunderbird flaps his wings."

"Tacante, my brother, there can be no more fighting. Look around you. Listen as the iron horse thunders past Platte River. Look at the towns rising from the prairie. Our father, Hinhan Hota, knows it's hopeless. He's set aside his lance. Can't you?"

"My medicine comes from the heart of the people," Tacante explained. "I can never be a man to look to myself. If Wakan Tanka says I must take up the warrior trail, then I will go."

"Won't be a Powder River fight this time," Louis warned. "Not with these new rifles. The soldiers have Gatling guns that shoot hundreds of bullets in an instant. No Lakota charge can survive that. Winter will find you alone on the plains. Who will feed the little ones? Don't ride to your death, Misun."

"I only go to hunt," Tacante said, gripping Hinkpila's hands. "And if I die, perhaps Itunkala will bring my sons to be raised by you in the old way."

"The old way's dead," Louis said, sighing.

"Then I am dead, too," Tacante replied mournfully.

"It's a sad world without brave heart hunts, Tacante."

"Full of blind, heartless people."

"Philip can manage the store a bit. I can spare some time to hunt our uncle Tatanka."

"It will be a remembered hunt."

"One of the last," Louis said sorrowfully.

"Yes, I fear," Tacante replied.

Louis rode along on the buffalo hunt, but they had poor success. Tacante had no spirit dreams, and Tatanka proved elusive. Finally the brother-friends settled for hunting elk in the hills.

"The good hunting days are behind us," Louis said finally as he saddled his horse and prepared to return to the fort. "Be careful, Misun," he added, passing into Tacante's hands two boxes of precious shells for the Winchester.

As Louis vanished behind the far horizon, Tacante felt a chill in spite of the blazing summer sun. Again he built the sweat lodge, and as the steam choked the bitterness from his heart, Tacante prayed for Wakan Tanka's help.

"I'm nothing," he cried. "I'm dust on the hillside."

He then climbed the nearby mountain and fasted three days. As he cut the flesh on his chest and danced, singing brave heart songs, he prayed for a vision.

Tatanka came at last to his dreams. Bull Buffalo limped across a plain littered with the bleaching bones of his thousand brothers. A woeful cry filled the air.

"Gone are sacred buffalo," the words called. "No more do my thunder hoofs shake the plains. The two-legged creatures have struck me down. Now comes the starving."

The words echoed through Tacante's dream, shaking him awake. He rose, light-headed, feeling as though a wall of gloom was falling upon him.

He spoke only to Hokala of the dreaming.

"Yes, Brother, it's a sad day for the Lakotas," Badger remarked grimly. "Long have I carried the lance of the Tokalas. Soon I will stake it in the ground and fight my last battle."

But there was good hunting still in the Big Horn country. The stolen road was quiet, and many elk and antelope grew fat on the good grass. The drying racks were full, and many fine robes waited to stave off the chills of winter.

Tacante soon merged his small band with the Oglala camps of his old friend, Sunkawakan Witkotkoke. The Big Horn country was full of Lakotas, and there were many Dakotas and Sahiyelas, as well. In spite of the deep snows and the frigid winds that came that winter, warmth flooded the lodges of the people. Old friends shared brave heart tales, and the young men boasted of their fine ponies and sure aim. Winter, too, passed.

Snow still clung to the earth when Crazy Horse moved his camp to Powder River. Other bands were nearby, and for once the people felt safe. They were far from Platte River and the wasicun forts. There was good food to eat. Fires warmed the lodges and cast off winter's gloom.

Tacante was enjoying a rare contentment when the camp crier announced the arrival of visitors. The Heart rushed out to see who had come. His face lit with a smile when he beheld Hinkpila clumsily dismount from an overburdened mule. With Louis was the spectacled brother Philip.

"Have you heard?" Louis called. "The army's orders?"

"We've heard nothing," Tacante answered. "Come inside. You are frozen and sure to need a warm drink."

Louis entered the lodge, but even as Hehaka worked to remove his frozen boots, the trader hurried to explain.

"It's General Crook," he said. "He's come to drive the hostiles back to the reservation."

"Back?" Tacante asked. "Reservation?"

"Was bound to happen, I suppose," Louis grumbled. "The peace commissioners couldn't make a new treaty, so they've reread the old one. Now, they say, all these lands beyond the Black Hills are needed for white settlers. It's time the Sioux take up farming on their reservation in Dakota. Those not at the agencies by January are considered hostile."

"January," Tacante said, recalling the strange wasicun names for the winter moons.

"Yes, it's past that now," Louis replied. "There's an army on the march. You have to hurry."

"Hurry where?" Itunkala asked, offering Louis a cup of hot bark tea. "This is our home."

"No, they've stolen Powder River and the Big Horns, too," Louis declared. "Too many to fight, Misun. Far too many."

"You say we must go back," Tacante said, considering the words. "Back to an agency that has never been home? What of Sunkawakan Witkotkoke? He's never lived there. This is the place where my sons will grow tall in the old knowledge. You say there are soldiers coming. Wouldn't they kill us anyway? They did at Blue Creek."

"I'd ride ahead and tell them you were coming in peace."

"Hinkpila, my brother, who would have ears for your words? It's not possible. The horses are hungry from winter starving, and the little ones are weak. I can't go. Better to fight than to watch the children freeze in their pony drags."

"I could take the little ones with me," Louis offered.

"You're frozen yourself," Itunkala pointed out. "How would Hinhancika endure such a trail?"

"When will the Star Chief Crook come?" Tacante asked.

"Soon," Louis said, frowning. "Very soon."

"Then we must put out the scouts."

Louis took the failure hard. He and Philip stayed but one night in Tacante's lodge, listening to the tales of the little ones and filling their bellies with meat. Next morning they left, hoping to warn others of the approaching danger.

It was all in vain. Even those bands who set off for Red Cloud or Spotted Tail could not erase the snow from their path. The snowblind moon of March found Two Moons and a band of Sahiyelas camped with Low Dog's Oglalas. The wasicun Star Chief Crook found both.

Bluecoats struck the camp hard, killing and burning. Warriors did their best to defend the helpless ones, but bullets flew like hailstones, and death was everywhere. Weary, near-naked survivors stumbled into Sunkawakan Witkotkoke's village with the terrible news. Soon the Lakotas were mounted and hurrying to avenge the killing. Crook's attack had failed already. The angry Sahiyelas and Oglalas had made a stand beside the river and turned the bluecoats back. Then others recaptured the stolen ponies and threatened the wasicuns. Now, with other Lakotas hurrying to join the fight, Crook returned to Fort Fetterman in failure.

"He did nothing but kill many innocents," Tacante grumbled as he gazed at the burned camp and the slaughtered people.

"Ayyy! He did much," Hokala objected. "The wasicuns have shown there is no going back. Two Moons, too, is with us. We'll make a good fight of it, Tacante."

Soon word came that the Hunkpapa Tatanka Yotanka, the Sitting Bull, spoke defiantly of a great gathering of all the people at the greasy grass.

"Come, join in the sun dance," criers shouted as they visited the many bands. "We'll be strong again."

"Hau!" the young men said. "Mahpiya Luta beat the wasicuns. Now will come our chance."

Tacante greeted this boastful talk with a bad face, for he dreamed often these days. No blanket of white covered the naked wasicuns now. Tacante dreamed only of a crying time on the plains.

Chapter Eighteen

Tatanka Yotanka was a famed medicine chief among the Hunkpapas. It was he who made the preparations for the sun dance. Even as the young men hung from the braided buffalo strips and howled their prayers, the Bull cut strips from his flesh and induced a great fever. While his spirit floated upon the wind, a great vision came to him of earless soldiers falling into the hands of the people. Sitting Bull's dreams were known to hold much wakan, great power. As he spoke of his dream, he explained it foretold of a victory that would soon be given to the brave hearts.

Tacante hoped it would be so, but he remembered Hinkpila's warnings. It would take a great victory indeed to rub out all the wasicuns, to kill the iron horse, and to recapture Paha Sapa from the hungry miners.

But as word passed among the many bands of the Bull's dream, more and more voices joined in the brave heart shouts. Warriors prepared their best shirts and cleaned their weapons. And the many who had gathered on the shores of the greasy grass stream, also called Little Big Horn River, were joined by agency Indians who had tired of scratching the earth. Lakotas and Dakotas spread their camps on the sandy banks. Even the cousin Nakotas, the people of the north who had fought the wasicuns so bitterly in Minnesota, appeared. Two Moons came, together with many other Sahiyelas tired of the broken promises of the wasicuns.

"Hau, we'll kill many bluecoats!" they boasted.

Never had Tacante seen such a gathering of the peoples. Hundreds of lodges rose in their mighty circles. To the east Sitting Bull, the great war chief Gall, and the rest of the Hunkpapas took a place of great honor. Beside them camped the Sihasapas and small bands of Dakotas, Nakotas, and Assiniboins. The Minikowojus spread their camp circle next. The Itazipos, the no-bow people, camped with the Ohan Numpas, the two kettles.

The Sicangus camped between the Itazipos and Oglalas, leaving the Sahiyelas on the far west. Tacante and Hokala set their lodges among the Oglalas, near where Sunkawakan Witkotkoke camped. The strange one more than ever walked his own trail, for he was preparing medicine for the fight all knew would soon come.

Already scouts brought word of the star chief Crook. Again he had set out from Fort Fetterman with many soldiers. To the north, past Yellowstone River, more bluecoats were marching. And from the Dakotas came the hated one, Long Hair Custer, who had violated Paha Sapa and caused that sacred place to be lost.

Tacante made many prayers. He wore the wakan bonnet of He Hopa, and he pounded buffalo horns to mix with the war paint of his brothers. Such paint bent the flight of bullets. Medicine charms were made for those too young to have fought before. The old men fashioned new arrows for sons and nephews, often using the wasicun iron of miners' pans or cooking pots. It was thought iron struck deeper into the hearts of these ignorant ones.

It seemed to Tacante as the long days of midsummer arrived that the bluecoats had lost their way. Crow scouts often traveled the country, and surely they had told the white men of the great encampment. Maybe it didn't suit the wasicuns to strike a village filled with so many fighters. Bluecoats preferred to strike at women and dogs, after all.

Soon, though, scouts brought word that Crook was near. It was not news to warm the heart. A thousand bluecoats, two hundred Crows, and many Snakes had gathered near Tongue River. Soon they would be at the throats of the helpless ones.

Crook had sent his Crows ahead, then followed. The bluecoat army moved slowly up Rosebud Creek, the foot soldiers riding mules and the horse soldiers going ahead. The whole force made camp on the creek where days before Lakota boys had swum.

"The wasicuns are close!" the criers shouted. "Now's the time to fight."

"Brave up!" the Tokala pipe carriers called. "We must ride to protect the helpless ones. Brave up!"

Tacante readied two war ponies and gathered a bag of wasna to sustain him. Itunkala soon appeared with two more horses.

"It's a good day to die, Ciye," he called.

"You're young," Tacante said, feeling less like Ciye, an older brother, and more like a grandfather.

"I'm a boy no longer," Itunkala insisted. "Today I win a name."

Tacante understood the Mouse's impatience, but sixteen snows made for a very short lifetime.

"Come then, but stay behind me. Here, use this," Tacante added, handing over one of his pistols.

"Hau!" Itunkala shouted.

Hokala and Waawanyanka led the Tokalas, and Tacante followed. Never before had he worn He Hopa's bonnet to a fight, but its powerful medicine would be needed to fight so many wasicuns.

"This time we will strike the wasicuns in their camp," Hokala cried. "They will be the defenseless ones."

"It's a long way," Tacante replied. "Night will find us not yet there."

"Then we'll rest our ponies beneath the chokecherry moon," Hokala said, waving toward where Sunkawakan Witkotkoke was assembling a band of Oglalas. Tacante motioned for Itunkala to follow, then led the way.

All night Tacante rode up Little Big Horn and across Wolf Mountain toward Rosebud Creek. It was nearing dawn when his band emerged atop a high bluff overlooking the soldier camp.

"Hau!" Hokala cried, pointing toward the dozing soldiers.

"Wait," Sunkawakan Witkotkoke urged. "We must put on our war faces, and the ponies want rest."

Tacante sighed, then silently rolled off his horse. He took his two ponies across the hillside to where the soft grass spread out beyond a small spring. He then lay down and chewed a bit of wasna. Itunkala joined him, and Hokala came along afterward. After devouring the dried meat and drinking from the spring, Tacante stretched himself out in the grass.

"Tacante, will it be a hard fight?" Itunkala asked.

"It's best to sleep," Tacante answered. "A weary warrior puts his companions into danger. Later we'll talk."

Tacante obediently lay on the ground beside his older brother. Tacante knew the young man wished to speak of battle, of death, but there was nothing, after all, to say. It would be learned quickly on the first brave heart charge.

It was but the briefest of rests. The sun hadn't even risen high in the sky when the sound of trotting horses stirred Tacante to life. All around him warriors were readying their ponies or painting their faces. Some put on their finest clothes, for they wished in death to be thought of as men of standing. Tacante followed the Horse's example and wore only a cloth breechclout and He Hopa's medicine bonnet. Hokala wore a fine shirt decorated with scalp hair while Itunkala stripped like his brother.

Tacante used the black ash paint on his face and hands, then colored his chest and arms with the sacred yellow of the sun. He made the horned sign of Tatanka on his chest and etched sacred thunder across his forehead. He then tied elk teeth behind his ears and took up the eagle whistle favored by Lakotas charging a determined foe.

"Misun, come here," Tacante called to Itunkala.

The Mouse hurried over, and Tacante tied elk-teeth charms behind his brother's ears. Tacante then spread ash across the Mouse's face and hands. The Heart felt proud of this boy, his mother's only other son, going to fight the wasicuns, but there was fear, too. Often it was the youngest who rushed ahead to die in a charge. There was no holding back a brave heart, though. All Tacante could do was paint the protecting yellow across the young man's narrow chest and grip him firmly a final time.

"You carry a good shield," Tacante said, noting the heavy round hump-hide shield made by Hinhan Hota. "Use it well, little brother, to keep harm away."

"Hau, I will!" Itunkala cried.

Now, as the Lakotas collected their ponies, shots broke the stillness of the early morning air. To the north a party of Crow scouts raced toward the protection of the wasicun camp. Behind them came a howling whirlwind of Lakotas.

For a brief time Tacante sat atop his horse and waited to see what the soldiers would do. The air was sweet with the scent of plums and cherries, and the hillsides exploded with color. It was a wondrous fine place. Soon the stain of blood and the odor of death would transform that scene.

The soldier chiefs hurried to form lines. The foot soldiers scrambled up the heights, but the ground was so rough and broken that instead of forming one line on the high ground, the bluecoats found themselves collected into several knots here and there. Wherever there was a gap, the brave hearts charged.

Tacante followed Sunkawakan Witkotkoke toward a line of horse soldiers, blowing through his eagle-bone whistle with the others. The sound unnerved the bluecoats, but they didn't flee. The Horse then raised his Winchester high above his head, screaming the old war cry, "Hau, Lakotas, it's a good day to die." The Oglalas howled in response and blew their whistles. In an instant they followed their strange one toward the bluecoats.

It was a fight unlike those Tacante had known. The Lakotas charged, fought hard, then pulled back. Then the wasicuns did the same. Back and forth went the charges. A man or two would fall each time, but no line was broken. The wasicuns had good guns, but they were poor shots atop racing horses. Where the foot soldiers formed lines, though, the Lakotas met with a withering fire that dropped many good ponies and sent good men to the other side.

Gradually the bluecoats seemed to take command. A Sahiyela charge was swept back by murderous rifle fire, and the soldiers rushed forward, cutting down stunned warriors trapped beneath horses. A brave deed was performed then by a young woman. Her brother, Comes in Sight, had his horse killed, and now he was in danger from a band of Crows. The girl howled like a demon and put on a bad face as she rushed to her brother's side. The surprised Crows held back from this phantom, and Comes in Sight was rescued.

By now many of Tacante's companions had shot away their bullets. Itunkala had no cartridges or lead for his pistol and had turned to the bow. Tacante had only a few shells with him for the Winchester, and he tied the good rifle behind him and took up the old ash bow as an example to the discouraged ones. But arrows were little good against men firing rifles. Lakotas fell wounded. Soon they satisfied themselves with driving the enemy, especially the Crows, from the fallen so they might escape.

As the thinning Lakota line began to waver, Sunkawakan Witkotkoke rode into their midst.

"Brave up, kolas," the Horse called. "Remember the helpless ones. Come with me. It's a good day to die!"

Hokala shouted as well.

"I'm a fox," he sang. "I'm supposed to die. If there's anything difficult, if there's anything dangerous, that is mine to do."

So saying, Hokala jumped from his horse and drove the sacred lance of the Tokalas into the earth. Itunkala knew of the lance bearer's oath, and the young man jumped down to join Badger. Others followed, and Tacante finally tied his horse to a cottonwood and hurried to his friends. Brave heart songs rose from the powder smoke as a band of Crows rushed the line. Arrows swiftly reached out and struck at the enemy. The Crow leader fell dead, and three of his followers retreated, wounded.

"Hau, Crows are afraid!" Hokala shouted. "Come and fight us if you aren't women!"

The Crows went to attack a band of Hunkpapas, though, leaving a line of bluecoats to deal with the Tokalas and their lance bearer.

Now came a hard fight. The soldiers fired a deadly volley into the Lakotas, but the medicine bent the bullets so that they struck short. When the soldiers moved closer, Tacante gave a yell and led the Lakotas in a foot charge. He struck down a two-stripe with his bow and drove a knife into a hairy-chinned wasicun. Now the Heart took his only scalp of the battle, though he counted other coups.

There were but fifteen Lakotas in that charge, but they sent fifty bluecoats running for safety. Victory shouts chased the bluecoats up a ridge, and all who saw it agreed it was a good charge.

Crazy Horse now drove the Lakotas on with brave heart shouts. He himself rushed in on horseback to rescue fallen warriors or cover a retreat. Sadly he looked at the tired horses and the weary warriors.

"Go down to the creek," he suggested. "The horses can drink and rest. If the bluecoats follow, they won't see us."

"Hau!" Tacante shouted with fresh energy. The Horse was playing decoy again. Let the star chief's soldiers come down there and die.

Tacante himself pulled Hokala's lance from the earth and urged his true friend toward the creek.

"We're not running away," Tacante said. "We go to make the ambush."

"Then I will be a decoy," Hokala insisted.

Indeed, Tacante also stayed behind, though it was Sunkawakan Witkotkoke who drew most of the attention. With his shiny Winchester held high, he taunted the soldiers to come down and kill him.

"Come!" Tacante shouted. "Are you afraid?"

The Star Chief Crook began to get control of his soldiers then. Three Stars, as he was known, sent his horse soldiers down into the creek, and the Lakotas braved up. Soon their arrows would find targets, and many good horses would be theirs.

The Crows charged out of the cottonwoods and screamed their warning. Arrows knocked two Crows from their horses, and Itunkala rushed forward to count coup on the first. Hokala drove the point of his lance into the other and took his scalp.

The soldiers started into the narrow ravine, but now Three Stars ordered a halt. Perhaps he remembered the foolish eagle chief Fetterman and the hundred slain. Perhaps his heart was bad with all the killing. He drew his men back, and they returned to their camps.

"Many have died," Sunkawakan Witkotkoke declared, staring at the many bodies littering the banks of the stream and the sides of the ridges. "We'll wait here and guard the trail to our camp. Hau! This has been a good fight, Lakotas!"

Tacante and the others blew on their whistles so that a shrill cry seemed to rise from Mother Earth herself. It was a terrible thing to hear.

The wasicuns made no more charges. Some Crows and Snakes rode among the nearby hills and slew cripples. The Lakotas tended their tired animals and nursed the wounded. Tacante made the healing chants and ground windflowers over many wounds. He made a rabbit poultice for Waawanyanka, who had been cut by a Crow lance on the arm.

The midday sun stood high over the land, and some spoke of resuming the fighting. Most had done enough. Hungry and tired, their bullets used up, the Lakotas started to head back to camp. Some sang brave heart songs. Others hung their heads in shame, for many of the loud-talking agency Oglalas had jumped from their horses and run away. Mahpiya Luta's son had left his horse and then been whipped badly by Crows. He was young, but he had gone to battle wearing a great war bonnet of eighty feathers, and all his friends now scolded him for such a foolish thing. He also lost a good Winchester to the Crows.

Other young men were praised, though. Hokala reminded the Tokalas of how Itunkala had been the first to his side, and Tacante's brother spoke of his two coups. The Heart drew the young man close and examined the bullet holes in the Thunderbird shield. Twice the Mouse had walked in death's shadow, but the shield had proven its worth.

"Now we go home," Tacante said, recovering his spare horse and offering it to one of the unhorsed Hunkpapas.

"Surely Tatanka Yotanka was right when he saw a great victory for the Lakotas," Hokala cried. "We've beaten Three Stars."

As they slowly made their way down Rosebud Creek, Tacante wondered if it had been a victory. Many good men were dead, and still the soldiers remained on Rosebud Creek. But next day Waawanyanka, who in spite of his wound remained to watch the bluecoats, brought word that the soldiers had gone back south.

"Hurry, Lakotas," Sunkawakan Witkotkoke called. "We must find what can be used again."

Tacante, weary as he was, mounted a fresh horse and followed. Many boys came along, too, for there was no fighting to be done now. The Lakotas returned to collect discarded clothing, but more importantly to recover arrows and dig lead from trees. Many cartridge boxes had been cast aside as well, and there were iron shoes to be pried from the feet of the dead soldier horses. That iron would make many arrowheads.

"Hau!" Itunkala yelled, dressing himself in the shirt of a fallen three-stripe. Other boys discarded their breechclouts to try the wasicun trousers. Most were dissatisfied, though, and used only the leggings.

There was good canvas thrown from the tops of wagons, too, and many flat tin plates and forks. Tacante found a good Crow knife half buried in the dirt. But it was the lead and powder that proved most helpful. Many would employ their bullet molds or make powder cartridges those next days. The Lakotas would not be defenseless long.

Chapter Nineteen

The great village of the Lakotas, Dakotas, and Sahiyelas passed a somber three days of mourning. Many brave hearts had fallen to the bluecoats of Three Stars, but this time the helpless ones were protected. Burial lodges were set up on the far bank of Little Big Horn, although many of the younger men were buried in the high country overlooking Rosebud Creek. The wounded were provided for by the healers, and Tacante's help was sought often.

Otherwise the camp was alive with the stories of bravery. Hokala was looked upon as a leader by the young Oglalas, for all respected a man who staked himself to the earth in defiance of the enemy. As for Tacante, all knew the power of the horned bonnet and elk-tooth charms made wakan by Heart of the People.

It seemed for a time that good days might follow the fight with Three Stars Crook. New arrows replaced those expended in battle, and many new cartridges and lead balls were made. There was a scarcity of percussion caps used by the old rifles and most of the pistols, though, for they were impossible to make. Some of the rifles taken off the Crows and Snakes were made to use flints, but good flints were also scarce.

"Soon we'll fight naked, with only the cold steel of our knives to protect us," Tacante complained.

"Still we will win," Itunkala boasted. "The bull says the fight on Rosebud Creek was not the victory he saw. It awaits us yet."

Tacante frowned at such talk. The scouts spoke of other soldier bands coming from the north, and there was no forgetting Blue Creek.

"Rest easy, Brother," Waawanyanka said when Tacante prepared to scout the hills to the east. "If there are wasicuns coming, I will find them. Always we send men to keep watch."

Tacante trusted Watcher, but many of the scouts grew tired of watching the barren landscape and took off to chase Crow ponies. Trust was placed in Sitting Bull's dreams, and few cares were devoted to tomorrow's plight.

Tacante sang and danced and ministered to the sick during this time. Often he conducted the Inipi rite, for men who rode into battle required strong purification. When not thus employed or off hunting fresh meat, he oversaw the instruction of his sons.

"You've taught me to use the bow, Ate," Tahca Wanbli said when Tacante praised the boy's skill. Not many youths could hit the elusive rabbit with the first arrow at such a tender age. "Soon I'll ride to war with you and Itunkala."

The notion soured Tacante, and he went into the hills to think. Two nights he stayed there, praying for a vision. None came, and he returned to his lodge in disappointment.

It was a fine, bright day, and Tacante paused briefly to watch boys chasing each other in the river. Itunkala was there, shouting and running down the younger boys. The older ones found Mouse as wiry and tough as old buffalo hide. For a moment young men of seventeen and eighteen summers ceased to be grim-faced warriors. Their taunts and laughter as they made mock charges through their younger comrades brought back warm memories to Tacante's heart.

Soon Tahca Wanbli would be among them. To think that he who was only yesterday a tiny child bouncing along in the pony drag would be a broad-shouldered boy soon, holding horses while his father and uncle engaged the wasicuns! Ah, that was a notion to age even a brave heart.

Tacante crossed the river slowly. As he gazed upon the wakening camp, he felt great pride. He could see beneath the rolled-up lodge skins that here was a great and powerful host. His dread of a wasicun attack had grown those last days. A young Sahiyela had dreamed of the coming of long knives, and many of the grandmothers spoke of an approaching enemy. Old ones had the all-seeing eyes, and they were to be listened to. And yet, seeing the people strong and numerous, Tacante's fears waned. The sun dance had brought Wakan Tanka's help, hadn't it? Three Stars and the bluecoats were leaving.

"Hau, Tacante!" Itunkala called, pausing in his game to race to his brother's side. Without his Thunderbird shield and war paint, the Mouse looked young and thin.

"Misun, you're very wet," Tacante said, laughing as his brother rested a waterlogged hand on one shoulder. "Perhaps the horses would also like a drink."

"Ayyy!" Itunkala shouted, grinning crazily. "I will ask them."

"Take care, little brother," Tacante advised, gripping the Mouse's arms firmly. "The enemy's scent hangs in the air."

"Hau!" Itunkala howled. "We'll have another fight then."

As Itunkala hurried to where he'd piled his clothes and dressed himself, a party of horsemen splashed along the banks of Little Big Horn. Tacante recognized Waawanyanka among them. Here were scouts come back from watching Three Stars. Watcher, in spite of his bad arm, refused to stay behind.

"It's a strange thing," Waawanyanka said, halting his horse when he reached his old friend. "The buffalo are gone from Rosebud Creek."

"And Three Stars?" Tacante asked.

"Ah, he's run away like a frightened rabbit, leaving only some Crows to watch."

Tacante nodded. The news should have cheered him. It didn't, and that was cause for more worry.

"Has anyone gone to the east to look?" Tacante asked.

"Some Sahiyelas are there, and we saw a band of Oglalas going away."

Tacante knew of this. Some of the bad faces were going back to Red Cloud. They were sure to send word if trouble lurked in that direction.

"It's good, kola," Tacante said finally. "Come, share my food. Hehaka always prepares too much."

"I will bring my family," Waawanyanka readily agreed. "After I see my horses fed."

152

"Leave them here," Tacante suggested. "Itunkala can see they have water, and the grass is good."

Waawanyanka climbed off his horse and handed the bridle to the Mouse, who was waiting behind his older brother, eagerly listening to each word. Now Itunkala was forced to turn to his labors. Tacante and Waawanyanka walked together past the Hunkpapa camp toward the lodges of the Oglalas beyond.

Thus the day began with Tacante's return to his camp. As he sat with Waawanyanka's family and his own three sons while Hehaka gave out pieces of stewed meat and turnips, he couldn't imagine a brighter, lovelier day to be alive. Cetan Kinyan climbed upon his father's knee and showed a fine brass buckle Itunkala had brought back from Rosebud Creek.

"Ate, you will take us to this place?" the boy asked.

"Itunkala talks of hunting there," Tahca Wanbli added. "Ate, can I take my bow?"

"Perhaps," Tacante said, holding Cetan Kinyan gently and smiling to the older boy. Hinhancika, the Little Owl, crawled over and nestled against his father's side, and Tacante wrapped an arm around him as well. Here was the future of the Lakota people. It was a comfort for a far-seeing man to look to the world beyond his nose.

Tacante devoted the rest of the morning to working hides. He gave the boys a chance to join in the work, and Tahca Wanbli joined eagerly. Cetan Kinyan and Hinhancika preferred to watch. Hehaka and her sisters had gone to dig turnips and pick a few late plums.

By midday Hehaka had filled her basket. She returned and made a soup. Itunkala had finished watering the horses, and he joined his brother's family for the meal.

"The Sahiyelas say soldiers are coming," Mouse told Tacante after the boys had gone off to chase a pair of camp dogs. "Many omens say it's so."

"Then maybe you should keep some horses close," Tacante advised. "Scouts are out, though. The Sahiyelas are always fearful of attack. Too many remember Sand Creek and Washita River. Others suffered on Powder River when Three Stars struck Two Moons."

Itunkala set off to bring the horses. Tacante thought to ride out and have a look to the west, but a young Sicangu arrived with a swollen arm, and the Heart turned his medicine eyes to the boy's hurt. Tacante determined it was little more than the bite of a wasp, and he offered a prayer and spread a curing lotion on the arm. By midafternoon he was back at his lodge, working on the hides.

Suddenly a sharp cry shattered the calm.

"Upelo!" a voice cried. "Wasicuns!"

The words cut through the heart of every warrior. Tacante stared at a terrified young Sahiyela racing among the lodges, ignoring the old rules of entering a camp only from the east. Horses whined, and Tacante set aside his hides and walked calmly to his lodge.

"Ate, are the soldiers coming to kill us?" Cetan Kinyan asked.

"No one will kill you," Tacante promised young Flying Hawk. "You must have the brave heart, though. Stay here and guard our lodge. Obey your brother, and help Hinhancika. I must make my face ready for war."

Tahca Wanbli quickly took charge of his brothers and brought them inside the lodge. Tacante was smearing ash upon his face and hands. Hehaka brought the buffalo shield, then helped her husband tie the elk-tooth charms behind his ears.

"Ate, here's your rifle," Eagle Hawk said when Tacante finished painting his chest. "Fight well."

"I will," Tacante pledged as he gazed outside. His eyes searched for Itunkala, but the Mouse was nowhere to be found. Hokala stood waiting for his old friend, though, and no more time could be wasted.

"I need a horse," Badger said, looking at the four animals hobbled nearby. "Rees have struck our herd."

"Take the buckskin," Tacante said as he placed He Hopa's bonnet upon his head. "Has Three Stars come back?"

"He had no Rees," Hokala reminded Tacante. "The bluecoats are striking the Hunkpapas even now. Come!"

Tacante joined the Badger, and together they mounted their horses. Tacante left the other two, hoping Itunkala would bring them along later. By the wave of fleeing women and children, it was clear a hard fight was going on ahead. A Tokala might take his time to make medicine, but he couldn't wait for others before striking the enemy.

He and Hokala moved east through the fleeing helpless ones. Boys no older than Tahca Wanbli hurried guns to their fathers and brothers.

Women carried shields. Old men shouted encouragement and stood ready with bows should the wasicuns break the Hunkpapa line.

Tacante was angry. He recalled Blue Creek, and he wondered why the scouts should not have seen the bluecoats earlier. Ree scouts! This must be the army come down from Yellowstone River. Or Long Hair Custer! Ah, it was good there were so many Lakotas nearby.

"Kolas!" the calming voice of Sunkawakan Witkotkoke called. "Come and fight! Defend the helpless ones! Shoot your last arrow and fire your last bullet! Let no soldier reach our camp!"

The strange one, near naked as usual and painted eerily, with the red-tailed hawk dancing in his hair, rode his horse toward the river, calling for others to follow. The hailstones dotting his chest gave wakan to his words. Tacante and Hokala set off to follow their old friend. Others arrived as well, and soon a band of Oglalas and Sicangus hurried to join the fight.

Clearly the soldiers were in a bad way. The Hunkpapas had recaptured the pony herd, and many Rees lay cut down at the edge of the camp. Lakotas also lay in the dust, some of them shot down by many bullets. Others moaned from their wounds and urged the others on.

"Brave up!" a young Minikowoju shouted as he fought to halt the blood flowing from his belly. "Already I'm dead. I wait for you on the other side."

"Hau!" the Oglalas called to him. "It's a good day to die, brother."

As Sunkawakan Witkotkoke charged the bluecoats at the water's edge, a great cry rose up from the other Lakotas. "Sunkawakan Witkotkoke comes!"

What little resolve remained in the soldiers standing near the river melted like ice in the noonday sun. A pair of Rees tried to meet the charge, but Tacante's Winchester cut them down. A buckskin-clad scout was caught by the chargers and cut to pieces. The Oglalas tore through the enemy as a sharp knife cuts bear fat, and the soldier line broke. Soldier horses fled in panic while the bluecoats hurried up a nearby hill. It was hard going for men on horseback, and Tacante halted.

"Save your bullets!" Crazy Horse cried. "Wait!"

But it was no use. The fight was an individual thing now. Lakota charged bluecoat, dodged a bullet, and struck down the enemy. Or else the bluecoat took careful aim and shot down a brave heart.

One group of clever bluecoats was hiding in a ravine covered by heavy brush. The Lakotas tried to root them out, but a heavy fire met each charge. Finally some boys set fire to the brush. After a bit the wasicuns howled and cried. One ran out into the open, choking, with his arm smoking. A young Hunkpapa charged him and cut his throat.

Fire soon forced other bluecoats and a Crow into the open, and these, too, were killed. Tacante had been resting his horse, but he saw a large wasicun carrying a small flag lead two companions toward the hill where the other bluecoats had fled.

"Kill them!" someone cried. "Get that flag!"

Tacante charged up beside them. One wasicun pulled a pistol, but Tacante knocked it aside with his shield. He then fired his rifle into the face of the flag carrier, blowing him from his horse. Tacante clubbed a second soldier to the ground. Others escaped a moment before a rush of Sicangus fell upon them.

Tacante tore the flag from the slain soldier's grip, then drew a knife and cut away the bluecoat's scalp. As the Heart held up the flag, the second wasicun fell upon him.

"I'll kill you, you devil!" the soldier shouted, clawing Tacante's side as might an animal. Tacante threw the soldier off, then turned back and drove the blade of his knife into the wasicun's belly down to the hilt. The bluecoat's eyes rolled back, and he screamed as Tacante drove the blade up into the vitals. A small army of young men now descended on the scene, eager to count coup on the dead soldiers. Tacante took the scalp before stepping away to tend the deep scratches in his side and back.

Sitting Bull appeared then, calling out that these other bluecoats, the ones on the hill, should be left to tell of their cowardly attack and of the death it brought them.

"Wakan Tanka has given us these lives," the Bull said, bringing back to all the memory of his dream.

Tacante swallowed those words and tried to cast off the bad heart he had for the wasicuns. Perhaps the hundred had charged, and he could see around him many dead. The Ree scouts were cut down hard. Many horses were captured. It was a great victory.

"Tacante, my brother, you fought well!" Hokala called, holding up a scalp. Tacante held up his two, then tied them to his belt and draped the captured flag across his chest. All around, the small boys and women had come to strip and cut up the bodies.

Tacante managed to laugh at the wide eyes of the little ones gazing at the hairy bodies of the naked soldiers. He recalled how strange he had thought it to grow hair in such odd places. But there was little time to observe the hard-hearted cutting up of those foolish wasicuns who had charged the huge Lakota camp. A soldier horn was blowing from the far side of the village. More soldiers were coming down toward Little Big Horn, toward the Sahiyelas, attacking the west where Hehaka and the little ones waited helplessly.

"Hau!" Tacante shouted, turning his weary horse. He kicked the animal into a gallop and raced along. Hokala was soon at his side, as were many of the young Oglalas. Up ahead Sunkawakan Witkotkoke had already gathered a force to cut down these women fighters.

"Hurry!" the cry arose. "Protect the helpless ones."

"Hau, kolas!" Waawanyanka shouted as he rode up, his shield tied to his useless arm. "Our people are in danger !"

Up ahead, where the river crossing led to the Sahiyela camps, a great host was turning the bluecoats back toward a hogback ridge. Two Moons was closing in on the other side, hungry for revenge against the wasicuns for the attack on his going-to-the-agency camp.

"Come, brothers!" Sunkawakan Witkotkoke called, waving his companions onward. "Follow the Sahiyelas! Let none of these wasicuns escape our hands!"

Tacante echoed the call, for already the sting of his slashed back and side drove hatred into his heart. He saw the faces of the little ones waiting in their father's lodge, putting the brave faces on even as fearful shooting grew closer.

Then Tacante's horse stumbled, and he fell against the rocky ground violently. If Hokala hadn't turned to fend off the following warriors, the Heart might well have been trampled. Tacante shook off the pain and got to his feet, then turned toward his horse. Already it was screaming in agony, for both forefeet appeared lamed.

"Look!" Hokala shouted, and Tacante turned and watched a solitary young rider appear, riding swiftly with a second horse carried along behind. It was Itunkala, his youthful face painted grim black.

"Here's a horse, Brother," the Mouse said as he reached Tacante. "It's a good day to die."

"Hau, Itunkala!" Hokala yelled. "Let no bluecoat escape."

Tacante now took out his eagle-bone whistle and blew the shrill call. A hundred and another hundred whistles answered. The sound swallowed the screams of dying wasicuns and the brave heart songs of Lakotas and Sahiyelas. A whirlwind of painted warriors, most of them now creeping up the rocky ridge on foot, was driving the wasicuns back. Small bunches tried to form lines here and there, but torrents of bullets and waves of arrows cut them down.

Tacante, Hokala, and Itunkala arrived to find Sunkawakan Witkotkoke exhorting his companions toward a clump of soldiers atop the hill. Tacante saw a tall wasicun chief firing his pistol and shouting bravely toward a handful of companions. This soldier seemed familiar. Perhaps Tacante had met him at Red Cloud. Perhaps the bluecoat was among those riding Paha Sapa, trying to drive out the thieves. It didn't matter. Tacante climbed off his horse, raised the Winchester, and shot the soldier chief in the knee.

Itunkala shouted loudly. Then, before Tacante could halt him, Mouse whipped his horse and charged the wasicuns.

"Misun!" Tacante called, fighting to move the lever and advance a new shell into the firing chamber of his rifle. Now Itunkala was in the way. The young man fired an arrow into the heart of a soldier. Then a volley of rifle fire spun the boy from his horse.

"Ayyy!" Tacante screamed, rushing toward the enemy. Bullets struck the buffalo shield, peppered the ground around him, but they didn't strike flesh or bone. Tacante slammed the shield against the first soldier, then clubbed another with his rifle, and shot a third. Hokala drove the point of his Tokala lance into the wounded bluecoat chief, and the three remaining wasicuns, their nerve shattered by the Lakota charge, fled up the hill. They were swallowed up by a band of Sahiyelas.

Tacante drew his knife and stabbed one of the senseless bluecoats while Hokala finished the other. Then the two kolas moved to Itunkala's side.

"I killed an enemy of my people," the Mouse said.

Hokala cut away the bluecoat's scalp and placed it in Itunkala's bloody hand.

"It was a brave heart deed," Tacante told his brother as he cried inside. Blood trickled out of the young man's mouth, and the narrow chest that had seemed so small that morning at the river seemed even smaller pierced by a pair of bullet holes.

"You'll send the scalp to our sister?" Itunkala asked. "You'll tell Hinhan Hota he had two brave sons this day?"

"I'll tell them so that they may sing of you in the winter camps," Tacante promised, gripping the small hand of his brother.

Itunkala then softly sang his death chant as a haze clouded his eyes. "I never grew tall," the young man muttered as death ended his suffering.

"Ayyy!" Tacante screamed, turning in anger to seek out some enemy, but there was none. Already the firing on the hilltop grew faint, and the victory cries marked the end of the wasicuns.

"Wakan Tanka!" Tacante called, cradling the head of his fallen brother. "Hold close this brave heart. Ayyy!"

Tacante then slashed his chest, hoping the pain might somehow cast away the sorrow of his torn heart. Death hung over Little Big Horn like a cloud, for the wasicuns killed there were many. For Heart of the People, there was but one slain, though. He carried that solitary corpse in his bleeding arms, noting how light a burden it was. Here was a young man never grown tall, one who walked the hard road with a boy's name. There should have been a feasting that night, and Tacante would have given a warrior's name to the brother who had earned it.

Now there would only be mourning.

Chapter Twenty

Tacante barely had time to wash his brother's body and dress it for burial. The bluecoats on the near hill remained, and many Lakotas were pressing them. Tacante had no more heart for war that day, and he devoted his time to treating the many wounded Oglalas and Sicangus. The wasicuns had not died cowards. Many a bullet had found its mark, and the wailing of the women echoed across Little Big Horn like the eerie call of the great horned owl.

There were shouts of triumph, too, for over two hundred soldiers lay dead under the summer moon. Many Rees and some Crows had also fought their last battle. Young warriors recounted their coups, and not a few proudly presented scalps to sisters and mothers. Many good guns and fine horses were taken, and a band of Sahiyelas proudly wore the blue shirts of their dead enemies.

That night the women and boys prowled the battlefield, taking anything that was of use. Others cut apart the bodies in a savage manner, for there was little love among the Sahiyelas for these wasicuns. Some who had survived the fight at Washita River said these were the men who had laid old Black Kettle low, for they carried the scissor-tailed flags with the number seven. It was even said Long Hair himself was among the dead.

As Tacante cut bullets out of bone and muscle or sang the healing chants over cut thighs or bruised heads, he didn't think of the hogback ridge blooming with the strange white bodies. His heart was full of sadness for the brother who would never again ride at his side.

Tahca Wanbli, Cetan Kinyan, and Hinhancika spoke little of the stiff body of Itunkala. Hokala had taken them amid the cottonwoods to cut scaffold limbs, and they had escaped long enough to visit the battle hill. Eagle Deer had recovered a fine leather belt and a box of Winchester shells from the body of a wasicun scout. The young boys contented themselves with snatching green picture papers and shiny buttons.

Tacante greeted their return with stern words, for it wasn't right to accumulate possessions while mourning an uncle.

That night, as Tacante lay on his buffalo hides, he noticed the children moaning in their sleep. Hinhancika thrashed about with his arms as if fighting back the enemy, and Flying Hawk, who was always the quiet one, screamed out in the night.

"Ate, I saw a head coming at me," the boy said, clutching his father's side.

"Brave up, Cetan Kinyan," Tacante urged. "It was only the dead head of an enemy." It took a long time to quiet his son's terrors, and Tacante knew the cause. Some of the older boys had taken heads of the enemy to kick around the camp. Better a rawhide ball had been used! It was wakan to strike the enemy, but to call down the ghosts of the enemy onto one's camp was folly.

By morning the moans of the wounded and the sobs of the mourning were not the only sounds on Little Big Horn. Scouts called out alarm that more soldiers approached from the north. The air was full of evil odor, for the dead turned foul under the summer sun.

"We must leave!" Waawanyanka cried. "There are no bullets for our good guns, and our arrows are all shot away."

Tatanka Yotanka already had the Hunkpapas breaking down their camp. Sunkawakan Witkotkoke painted his face and tied up his horse's tail, but there were few with the bad heart for more fighting.

"Tacante, you will come?" the Horse asked. "We'll decoy them into ambush and strike them down."

"I cannot," Tacante explained, for he was in mourning, and he'd set aside his rifle. "I go to bury my brother."

There were many dead to see to, and finally it became clear this new band of wasicuns faced no attack. Even the bluecoats on the near hill were safe from Lakota arrows. There would be no fighting that day.

"Upelo!" a Sahiyela crier called out. "Upelo!"

"They're coming to kill us!" women shouted.

"They are still far away," Waawanyanka spoke in a calming voice. "Brave up, Lakotas. There is time to tend our dead."

And so Tacante and his brother-friends took Itunkala deep into the hills. There they placed him on a scaffold overlooking the river. The distant Big Horn peaks seemed to watch over the young man, and Tacante made the many prayers and cut his chest again to take on the suffering of the traveling soul.

Tahca Wanbli drew out a small knife and cut the skin of his chest so that blood flowed.

"Itunkala was my father's brother, my father by blood," the boy said somberly. "I mourn him."

Tacante watched with pride as the younger boys also made the giving up of blood. Then the Heart led the way back to the camp.

Madness had now descended upon Little Big Horn. Everywhere people were tearing down lodge skins and packing up belongings.

"Soldiers come," many said. And when Waawanyanka rode to see if it was true, he hurried back with the dreaded news.

"They come like ants upon the plain," Watcher warned. "Many. We must ride hard."

Tacante looked at the tall poles of good pine and sighed. It was hard work cutting new poles. But pony drags would slow the escape, so there was nothing else to do. He folded the tough buffalo-hide covering and tied it to a packhorse. He then gathered the other belongings and packed them as well. It was good to be a man of many horses, for even Hinhancika rode a pony by himself as they headed away from the stinking place. Little Big Horn was left to the wasicuns, but Tacante would always carry in his heart the memories of triumph and despair.

It wasn't right to travel when in mourning, and Tacante led a small band of friends and relations into the Big Horn country. There they camped and sang the sad songs. Hokala killed a deer, and there was fresh meat to bring strength. Tacante erected a sweat lodge, and Inipi offered purification. But nothing cut away the sadness.

162

The sun rose and fell three times before Tacante readied his small band for the hard trail. By then soldiers were everywhere, searching all the country for Lakotas. The bluecoats from the north set loose armed parties of Crows, and Three Stars stopped his flight and searched Powder River. Tacante made camp in caves, making no fire for fear the Crows would catch the scent. Now was a running time. The Winchester knocked down elk or antelope to fill the hungry bellies, but the bullets grew to be few, and Tacante often made arrows.

"Once we were a great host," Hokala grumbled as the chokecherry moon faded into memory. "Now we, who killed our enemies, run from them like hares chased by hungry wolves."

"Ah, we are chased by wolves," Tacante said, gazing upon the wary eyes of his sons. "Hinhan Hota was right. There is no fighting the wasicuns. Kill two, and three come instead."

As always in such times of great trial, Tacante climbed the mountainside until he found a place where he was alone with the sky. There he prayed and starved himself until a vision appeared.

At first the dream seemed familiar. There was Tatanka thundering across the plains. He seemed to bellow fiercely as he trampled beneath his hoofs many wasicuns. Then came a whirlwind of bullets, and Bull Buffalo fell, bleeding.

"Cry for me, Tacante," the spirit whispered. "And for yourself. Our time is finished."

Beyond the whirlwind rose the steep sides of Mato Tipila Paha, the sacred Bear's Lodge. When Tacante awoke from his dreaming, he knew it was the place they must go. There, in that sacred place, perhaps peace waited.

So it was that Tacante led the way eastward, across the Big Horn Range, past Powder River, on through the yellow grass prairie once ruled by the buffalo. Bear's Lodge reached out to the fugitives, called them. There Tacante had joined the sun dance. Surely Wakan Tanka still dwelled in that holy place.

They spent the rest of summer evading the wasicuns and the Ree and Crow scouts. The horses were exhausted, and the little ones weak and thin. Winter would come soon, and where were the stores of wasna to sustain them? Hardly a day did Tacante know the same camp, and cook fires were lit only in the daylight. Even then, no thought was given to drying meat. The risks of discovery were far too great.

Then, even as Tacante's despair darkened his somber face, Waawanyanka's sharp eyes detected riders on the plain ahead.

"Lakotas!" Hokala called.

"Sunkawakan Witkotkoke!" Waawanyanka shouted. The Horse was there.

Crazy Horse was glad to welcome the lost ones to his camp. This was not the great band of Oglalas that had camped at Little Big Horn. Many had returned to Red Cloud's agency even before the fighting, and others had gone afterward. Those who remained were far thinner than summer usually found them.

"The wasicuns chase us hard," the Horse explained. "We would fight them, but we have no bullets for our guns, and arrows cannot find the dark hearts of the bluecoats from far away."

Tacante thought, too, that more and more of the older warriors were turning their faces away from the death another fight was sure to bring.

If Tacante's voice had carried weight with the Oglalas' council, the band might have erected their lodges at Bear Lodge. Sunkawakan Witkotkoke turned north, into the low hills, where many peaceful Lakota bands made their autumn camps. Scarcely had they stretched the lodge skins over such cottonwood and willow poles as could be cut than the sounds of gunfire carried across the hills. Tacante listened glumly to the faint noise, knowing surely here was another Lakota camp struck hard. It was bitter news, for that ground was part of the reservation set aside for the people at Fort Laramie long ago.

Soon riders appeared with dread news.

"Soldiers have attacked our camps. They killed American Horse and many brave hearts," a young man said. "Come, help us fight!"

"Who will follow the Tokala lance?" Hokala cried, and many howled their eagerness to punish the wasicuns.

It took a short time to paint faces and tie up the ponies' tails. Then Sunkawakan Witkotkoke led his Oglalas toward the threatened village.

Tacante had hoped it was perhaps Crow scouts who had attacked American Horse's village. But as the Oglala riders approached the battle, it was clearly a big soldier force. Women and little ones fled over the rough ground that led to Slim Buttes, where American Horse fell.

And when the Lakotas arrived, they saw to their disappointment that Three Stars and a wasicun army were busy burning the lodges and killing such Lakotas who remained to fight.

"I am a fox," Hokala began to sing as he waved his lance high over his head. And even as he sang of the difficult things a Tokala must do, Badger led a charge against a party of horse soldiers.

It was a hopeless thing, fighting so many with little more than bows and arrows to answer bullets. But a brave heart never hung back when his kola charged. Tacante followed, screaming a war cry and then blowing his eagle-bone whistle. The bluecoats turned and dismounted. They lifted their rifles to their shoulders and unleashed a wicked volley at the charging Oglalas. A young man called Rushes Ahead fell first. Then No Paint died. Hokala continued on, for his medicine bent the bullets from his chest. He struck the center of the bluecoats and pierced one soldier with the lance. Then his horse went down, and he stood alone among many enemies.

"Ayyy!" Tacante screamed as he raced to rescue his friend. Hokala planted the lance, though, and he dove into the bluecoats with a slashing knife. They must have thought a demon was among them, for they fell back, stunned. Then one fired his pistol into Hokala's back, and another clubbed Badger's head.

Tacante managed to drive the enemy back from Hokala, but the life had already left when the Heart lifted Badger's body.

"Here is a brave heart!" Tacante shouted, taking the lance from the earth. But as he placed Hokala atop the horse and led it from the battle-scarred village, Tacante wondered what such a good man had died for. The camp remained in the hands of Three Stars, and even Sunkawakan Witkotkoke's fiery words could not move the Oglalas to retake it. Too many, it seemed, had died already.

Chapter Twenty-One

Not since Itunkala's death had Tacante known such pain. All the best and bravest among the warriors seemed gone now. Others would surely follow, for winter was a starving time. Now the Oglalas had more helpless ones to feed, and the good hunting moons were behind them.

"There will be game on Tongue River," Sunkawakan Witkotkoke said confidently. "There we'll be beyond the reach of long knives."

Tacante wondered. In their flight from Little Big Horn, the Lakotas and Sahiyelas had often set the prairie afire. With no grazing, the buffalo and elk had fled that good country. It was a long way to go, and the chill wind was already making itself felt.

"I have a wife and daughter, and a brother's wife and son to watch over," Waawanyanka told Tacante when the camp started west. "I'm tired of running. My heart is sad for all the dead young men, for the slaughtered children. My fighting days are ended."

Tacante gazed upon Watcher, the faithful one, he who was forever vigilant. Wakinyela and their little girl stood near, as did Sunlata and Hokala's boy. There was no fire in their eyes. Yes, the fight was over.

"Hinhan Hota is at Sinte Gleska," Tacante told his brother-friend.

They would be welcomed at Spotted Tail, given food and clothing. It wasn't such a far way.

"Come with us," Waawanyanka urged.

"I am the Heart of the People," Tacante answered. "I know the curing songs. I can't turn away from the sacred road."

"Ah, my brother, can you be sure it doesn't lead you to your father's lodge?"

"Yes," Tacante said, sighing. "It's never the easy path. It requires more suffering."

If that was true, the suffering soon came. It was a long, difficult journey across the stump grass to Powder River and the Big Horns beyond. Never was there a time when the fear of attack was not heavy on the warriors' minds. Tacante prayed often for visions, but Tatanka was dying, and he spoke only of more dying.

The winter moons found Three Stars Crook again prowling Powder River. While the deer were shedding their antlers, a new wasicun wolf swept down on Dull Knife's Sahiyelas. This was Mackenzie, he who had killed the ponies. In a fight against the southern people, he had captured a winter camp and shot the pony herd. This time his men shot mostly Sahiyelas, but they also burned the lodges, the blankets, even the winter meat. These Sahiyelas rushed to the safety of Sunkawakan Witkotkoke's Oglala camp nearby, and what was already in short supply was cheerfully shared.

Tacante gazed sadly at his frayed lodge skins and ordered them cut apart. Three pieces were made, and two Sahiyela families also had protection against the wind.

"Ate, our tipi is so small," Tahca Wanbli observed as he huddled with his mother, brothers, and father in the square hut stretched over willow limbs. "No longer can we burn a good fire."

"We will stay warm," Tacante promised, avoiding the probing eyes of Hehaka and the little ones. "We have good elk and buffalo robes, and the lodge skin is strong against the snow."

"And if the soldiers come?" Cetan Kinyan asked.

"Then I will fight them and chase them across Powder River," Tacante boasted. "When did Sunkawakan Witkotkoke ever lose a fight to Three Stars?"

The questions were often repeated as it grew colder, and the days were rare when there was enough to eat. Hinhancika grew to be a feeble shadow, and Tacante often held his little sons tightly and rubbed warmth into their frail bodies.

Under the terrible moon the unthinkable occurred. Bluecoats struck the camp. It was the Bearcoat, Nelson Miles, who found the Oglala camp. Already he had punished Gall's Hunkpapas and sent Sitting Bull hurrying to the Grandmother country. Now he had come to kill Crazy Horse.

They came out of a heavy mist. Horses snorted steamy breaths as the riders surged through deep snowdrifts. Bullets tore through lodges, striking the helpless. Terror flooded the land. Tacante threw on an elk robe and covered his face with ash from the fire. Then, using the old ash bow made in his youth, the Heart rushed out to greet the bluecoats.

No buffalo shield bent the bullets, and no elk teeth blinded the enemy. Tacante was a lone Lakota standing in the open, ready to be killed. Three soldiers tried. The first took a bullet in the chest and fell bleeding into the snow. Tacante grabbed his horse and met the second enemy mounted. The wasicun tried to fire his pistol, but the ash bow knocked it aside. Then the bow delivered a hard blow to the neck, unhorsing the wasicun.

The third soldier was a two-stripe, and he made no effort to close with a Lakota so practiced in the art of battle. Instead, he aimed his rifle and fired. It shattered the bow, and Tacante looked at the broken pieces in dismay. Then, screaming like a diving hawk, he slapped the horse into motion and simply ran down the rifle shooter. The soldier fell, and his own horse killed him as it fell atop him.

Tacante watched as the Oglalas found their horses or took mounts from the soldiers. Soon the warriors were driving the soldiers back from the camp. Tacante found two running ponies and brought them to Hehaka.

"You must see to your mother and brothers, Tahca Wanbli," Tacante told his son. Already Hehaka had managed to gather the warm hides and what dried elk meat remained. Tacante climbed down and helped tie the belongings onto the horses. Then he lifted Hinhancika atop the first pony and then assisted Hehaka to climb up. Cetan Kinyan mounted the second animal.

"Ate, you'll need this," Tahca Wanbli said, handing Tacante his rifle and shield before following Flying Hawk onto the second pony.

"Thank you, Cinks," Tacante replied. He passed the rifle back, for it held but three shells now. ·

"But your bow is ruined," Tahca Wanbli objected.

"I have this," Tacante explained, holding up the pistol taken from the wasicuns on Powder River so long ago. "Now hurry to safety. I will stop the soldiers here!"

So it happened, for Bearcoat's men suffered greatly from the blinding snow and the numbing cold. They could not press the attack against the Horse's angry warriors. Finally they had enough, and the shooting died. Tacante rejoined his family.

"Hau, Ate!" Tahca Wanbli called. "You've taken a scalp!"

"Yes, we've punished them hard," Tacante said, sadly observing the shivering children.

"I'll miss our lodge skins," Cetan Kinyan whimpered.

"Maybe we'll find a good cave tonight," Tacante said, touching the Hawk gently on the shoulder. "And later we'll make a new lodge."

"And will the soldiers come to chase us from it, too?" Flying Hawk asked.

Tacante bowed his head under the hard gaze of this small son. For the first time he had no answer. He was no longer strong or wise enough to protect his family. Winter's claws tore at them. Could there be a darker time?

There could. As Tacante rode out to spy on the bluecoats, he caught sight of Three Stars's scouts. These weren't Rees or Crows. On the left were Sahiyelas, and on the right—Lakotas. In the lead was . . . no, it couldn't be. But it was. Waawanyanka was wearing a three-stripe blue coat. Now the people were hunting their own brothers.

Watcher wasn't the only familiar face Tacante spied that bitter winter. As Sunkawakan Witkotkoke's party eluded their pursuers, Hinkpila appeared. Louis and his brother Philip led six fine buckskin ponies and a pack mule laden with dried venison and flour and good blankets.

"Hau, brother!" Tacante called as he and three young men met the two traders.

"Hau, brother," Louis replied. "I'm glad to see you still have your hair."

"You may not have yours so long riding this country alone," Tacante scolded. "Many would kill for the goods you carry."

"It's not by accident I've found you," Louis explained, speaking in English the other Lakotas could not comprehend. "Colonel Miles sent dispatches to Fort Fetterman, and Philip got wind of them. We came out this way, and who did we meet but Watcher. He said you were with Crazy Horse."

"I'm not the only one."

"No, but I speak Lakota fair when there's need, and Wicatankala beaded me a shirt in the old fashion. I thought mentioning your name might help, too."

"Why have you come, Hinkpila, Istamaza?"

"To bring you home," Louis answered. "Your sister worries. The fighting's finished, Tacante. Over. Surely you can't hope to escape when so many are after you."

Tacante only frowned. He dismissed his companions, then led Hinkpila and Istamaza to the snow dwelling that served as a home.

"I didn't know how hard things were," Louis whispered when he joined Hehaka and the little ones around the fire. "Look at the little ones, Brother. They grow thin. Let me fill their bellies. Come back to Laramie. We'll hunt the elk and share the good stories of better days beside a warming fire."

Tacante watched Tahca Wanbli's eyes light up. Hinhancika crawled over and curled close to his uncle. Cetan Kinyan sat with Philip Le Doux and babbled about the many soldier fights.

"Tacante, come in," Louis pleaded.

For the first time Hehaka turned to her husband. Her eyes echoed the plea.

"You're my brother," Tacante said, dropping his chin to his chest. "I can't provide for my family's needs as I once could. Hinkpila, take them into your lodge as my father once welcomed you. Give them food and clothing and shelter."

"And you?" Louis asked.

"I stay with Sunkawakan Witkotkoke. I walk the trail to its end."

A heavy silence filled the frigid hovel the remainder of the night. And when Louis and Philip carried Hehaka and the children away that next morning, Tacante was already preparing his death song. Life had lost its sweetness, death its terror.

Chapter Twenty-Two

The world is a circle, and a man's trail is constantly turning back upon itself. In the despair of winter, Tacante painted his face black and prepared to fight a last battle. It wasn't to be. Louis Le Doux wasn't the only brave heart to speak of setting aside the lance and coming to the reservation. Sinte Gleska, the Spotted Tail, came to urge Crazy Horse to give up the ghost trail. Here were strong words well spoken. And with the hunger of a starving winter leaving the people weak and fainthearted, many followed the Tail to fight no longer.

In the end, it was Three Stars Crook who convinced the Horse it was time to end the hard fight. The soldier chief spoke of a new agency for the Oglala strange one, a fine place on Tongue River, where the elk grew tall and strong, and the air was crisp and clear. It wasn't a stinking place like the flatlands where Red Cloud and Spotted Tail waited for the wasicun handouts. There were no soldier forts in that country.

Late in the spring Sunkawakan Witkotkoke rode into Camp Robinson, near Red Cloud's agency. With him were eight hundred horsemen, riding proudly in their finest clothes. Streaming feather tails flowed from bonnets of eagle feathers. Faces were painted red and yellow and, yes, black. War songs filled the air, and for a moment soldiers ran about as if an attack was expected.

It was all a show. Crazy Horse wished everyone to know he wasn't a beaten warrior dragged in starving to a jail. No, here was a great warrior, unconquered, yet ready to hand over his weapons to make the good peace.

Tacante rode in that line of warriors, but his face bore red paint. There was no bad heart for this peace. Already he'd learned from Louis that Hehaka and the little ones were with her father at Red Cloud. Soon Tacante would again know the warmth of his wife's tender touch and the admiring eyes of his sons. Or so he hoped.

"It's time for peace," the Horse had said. "The buffalo are dead, and so are many brave ones. I have no heart to see more die."

Tacante knew those feelings. They were his own. As he laid his Winchester and the old Colt pistol in the pile of guns, he knew his warrior days were at an end. He had yet to walk the earth thirty summers, but he was an old man.

Hehaka noticed the change when he greeted her beside her father's lodge. Wanbli Cannunpa had that same beaten expression on his face. Tahca Wanbli leaped into his father's strong arms, though, and howled in delight. Cetan Kinyan ran over as well, his dark eyes shining with delight. Even Hinhancika, who had departed as little more than a painted skeleton, hugged his father tightly and boasted of his restored strength.

"Life here is not like the old free days," Waawanyanka explained later. "Some of the young men, as I did, ride as scouts for the soldiers. Others take to strong drink. We eat the stringy Texas cows, and my teeth hunger for pte, sacred buffalo cow."

"Why have we surrendered, then?" Tacante asked. "Why have we let them put us in this reservation cage?"

"Why is Tatanka dead?" Waawanyanka asked. "Who has answers? The children grow tall and strong, and we have buried no brothers here. Perhaps it's enough."

Tacante wondered. He wasn't the only one.

As the moons came and went, and Three Stars's promised reservation on Tongue River didn't come, Sunkawakan Witkotkoke spoke often of returning to the old ways. There were Powder River and the Big Horns waiting. Who could stop the Horse if he chose to ride there?

It was spring, and scouts had spotted buffalo. All the young men wanted to go to hunt them, and as the herd was on reservation land, the treaty allowed such a hunt. But when Sunkawakan Witkotkoke prepared to leave the agency, soldiers and Lakota police were sent to stop him.

"Come with us!" they shouted, taking him in their hands. As they dragged him toward the iron-box jail, the Horse gave a shout and struggled to free himself. A soldier or one of the Lakota police used his bayonet. Cold, cruel steel pierced the Horse's flesh, and he sank to the ground, mumbling his death song.

So died Sunkawakan Witkotkoke, slain in the shadows of a dark hour. Many mourned his passing.

"You cannot cage a hawk," Tacante told his sons. "His pain is over now."

Tacante searched his own heart for direction. With Hehaka, he tried to bring on a dreaming, but there was no wakan on the agency. He longed for the high places and the hunting.

"What brave trail will my sons walk?" Tacante asked Hinhan Hota when the Owl came for a visit. "Paha Sapa is full of wasicun towns. Pe Sla and Bear Lodge are gone. Where will we perform the sun dance? How will Wakan Tanka know his children?"

"Ah, who can see the wind?" Hinhan Hota replied. "Who can tell what tomorrow's sun will bring?"

Tacante gathered the boys together that night. He sat beside the fire, crafting a fine bow of river ash. As he worked, he spoke of how the first bow was given long ago by the Sky Father to a brave hunter. Tacante also told of Itunkala and Hokala.

"What will I hunt?" Hinhancika asked.

"Ate, how will I win a warrior name?" Tahca Wanbli asked.

Tacante had no answer. As he gazed around at the silent lodges, clothed in the amber shadow of the sinking sun, he wondered. For it seemed the old ways had passed. And now there was but the dying of the people left.